A Survival Story

by

John Rourke

1776PatriotUSA.com

Freedom – Firearms – Preparedness - Patriotism

DEDICATION

This book is dedicated to author and survivalist – Jerry Ahern. Mr. Ahern made an enormous impact on my life. As a teenager I read his book series, The Survivalist. Many hours were spent consumed with the adventures of John Thomas Rourke as he battled evil Communists and gangs of motorcycle riding brigands all while searching for his family after a nuclear war.

Jerry Ahern has left us but the effect he has had on my life and many others will carry forward.

Introduction

Welcome to **A Survival Story**.

What follows is a fictional daily journal written by "Jed".

Jed is a 39 year old man who lives in the small city of Rock Hill, South Carolina. Jed recently started thinking about his life and the many mistakes he has made. Jed has decided to start keeping a journal to organize his thoughts and try to understand not only where he has been but where his life is going. Jed begins this journal at a time in his life when he is considering whether he will ever meet "the one" and has just scheduled a trip to attend his 20 year high school reunion.

Jed is relatively physically fit. He enjoys working out with weights, takes martial arts, and rides his mountain bike periodically on some light trails. He would like to lose about 15-20 pounds but is not overly concerned about it. Jed is 5′ 10″ tall and 205 pounds with very short brown hair. Both his parents have passed and his younger brother Eric moved in with him a couple months ago. Jed has always felt the need to care for his brother since his parents are no longer around.

He has been an active survivalist for the last several years – especially since the economic troubles of 2008. He has stocked up on a lot of supplies with an emphasis on the basics of "beans, bullets and band-aids". The few people that know of Jed's concern for the future dismiss his "prepping" as a hobby - a fad. Jed takes it serious, however he is not fanatical about it and enjoys many of life's comforts like anyone else.

Jed recently purchased a 2014 black Jeep Wrangler 4-door – a rare splurge for himself. He hopes within the next decade to purchase several acres of land in the country and develop a small homestead. Until then.....he continues to work, stock away supplies, develop his small parcel of land, and hopes to have a family.

<u>Jed is one of the good guys</u>. He is patriotic and remembers growing up saying the pledge of allegiance and a prayer before lunch in school. He does not do drugs and drinks rarely. He judges people not by the color of their skin but by the content of their character. Politically, he is Conservative but feels most all politicians are crooks and dishonest. Jed is a Christian and believes in God but has never found a church that he felt comfortable in. He wants to change that.

In many ways Jed is just an average guy who will find himself in a very unique and challenging situation.

Here we begin....... a survival story.

June 18th   Starting something new.......

I am a little surprised I am doing this and no doubt would be made fun of my some of my friends. Keeping a journal? I decided to do this – to record my thoughts, my life on paper to clear stuff out of my head and if I ever have kids to have something to pass onto them. Maybe they can gain some kind of wisdom from me – who knows?

Well – I plan to write stuff every day but may miss a day or so every once in a while. Work gets busy, life gets busy.

What has been going on lately? Did a crazy thing and bought a new Jeep. Saved up and put a large amount down so my monthly payment would be low. A big event coming up in a couple weeks – my 20 year high school reunion. I am a bit nervous about it. Most everyone I went to school with I have not kept in contact with. I wish I had. I wasn't very popular and tended to be somewhat of a loner. Then there is the question of "M" – that's what I called Monica. We dated most of twelfth grade and it was pretty serious – then after graduation things just fell apart and I moved away. I wonder if she will be there. Will she be married? Kids? Likely of course. Not everyone has stayed single like me – just never found anyone. Ok – let's be honest here - I never found anyone to replace M.

OK. There is my first entry in "Jed's Journal." Going to watch a rerun of **The Walking Dead** before I hit the sack.

- Jed

June 19th   First of many clues.......

Work was terrible today. People just drive me crazy. I do not understand how two people can look at the same issue and have two totally different opinions. Well – I guess that is how this government got so screwed up. You have Democrats and Republicans that are always on opposite ends of issues thus nothing ever gets done right. Maybe I am exaggerating a bit – maybe not.

My brother Eric said I was a couple cans short of a six pack today. He saw several cases of the Mountain House foods stored in the spare bedroom. I let him live with me rent free and he is still unbelievably rude. He was spoiled rotten as a child and expects everything to just be handed to him. I guess I am not helping matters much by not forcing him to pay rent. Will change that soon.

Interesting news today that is getting me concerned. North Korea announced they were going to be performing two tests within the next few weeks. One was a long range missile "experts" say could reach the United States– or close. The other test was an underground detonation of a nuclear weapon. Increased sanctions against North Korea are being threatened and North Korea is saying that if that happens they will consider it an act of war. What a mess.

- Jed

June 20th   A date with Diane.......

Picked up a Kindle Fire today. It's pretty cool. I bought it on Amazon and downloaded a few books – mostly preparedness stuff. I wonder those that read my journal 20 years from now – what will they say about my interest in preparedness? Hopefully they will say I was crazy. I just think it makes sense to be ready in case of a power outage, some major disaster, or of course if aliens invade!

Spent some time in the garden after work. Cucumbers looking great and zucchinis are getting HUGE!! Bucket potatoes are almost ready to be harvested anytime. I continue to add to the compost pile with table scraps and a little grass from the lawn mower once in a while.
As usual it has been super hot and I water the garden daily at the moment. Hope we get some rain as a couple of my rain barrels are getting low. The gardens like rain much more than city water.

Had a third date with Diane. She is great, but not sure what the future holds. As usual I am looking too far forward AND too much in the past. Diane has two great kids from her first marriage and not looking to have a second marriage anytime soon. I seem to make her laugh and the chemistry is there – so far. Dating at almost 40 is not easy. Tonight we went to Outback. Great meal and great company. Great kiss as well!

I think she liked my new Jeep!

- *Jed*

June 21st   *A missile test is carried out.......*

North Korea carried out their missile testing and it actually worked. Reports say the missile is capable of reaching the United States. The President is threatening to withdraw aide sent for the people of North Korea. That's not all. They also conducted the underground nuclear test they promised. Big parade in the North Korean capital city flexing their military might. Not good. Most folks think countries like North Korea and Iran are of no threat to the United States. I disagree.

I am thinking of taking some money out of the bank and stocking up on more supplies. Yeah – preparedness stuff. The weather has been crazy for the past year or two and not getting better. Living in hurricane country it would probably be a good idea to increase my food stores. I am getting concerned about the economy, government debt, societal decay, and the world just isn't getting any safer. I have always kept quite a few supplies on hand but feel like I need to take it to the next level.

Hoping to go shooting over at Ben's this weekend. We are not really that close but seem to get a long good at work. Hoping to shoot my AR and Winchester 94 some.

- Jed

June 22nd   Come on little brother.......

Good day today – it's Friday. Got off work a little early and went to SAM's. I did it. I spent close to $1000 on food and some other supplies. Bought some more bags of rice, beans, quite a few canned goods, spices, etc. SAM's just started carrying some freeze dried food and grabbed some of that as well. Now I have to find some place to put it all. Eric thinks I am crazy but little brother will just have to deal with it since I let him stay at the house rent free.

I hope Eric is going to grow up some day. He seems to live life carefree and pays no attention to what is going on in the world. Sometimes when I am watching YouTube videos about the economy and preparedness, I think he is actually paying attention. I don't know. He seems to be doing OK with his "raised bed gardening" business I started for him. I take the appointments and he goes and builds the raised beds.

Heading to Ben's tomorrow. Need to hit the sack.

- Jed

June 23rd   Spent the day at Ben's.......

Good time at Ben's. Man – he has a nice set up. He lives out near Chester way in the country. His dirt driveway winds through the woods for probably 300 yards before you see his house. He set up a 100 yard shooting range near his barn and we shot there. Everything was sighted in pretty well. The Winchester 94 has open sights and I was able to keep shots on a pie plate. That is good for me.

Wonderful family Ben has. Great kids. His wife Carrie made the best tasting banana pudding I have ever had. He is really lucky. I am so jealous. Could Diane and I be like that some day? Maybe. Hell, I am a great catch!!! 39 years old. In decent shape. I am smart, make good money, outgoing, ...funny? I think so.

Ben has a large garden, a few cows, chickens, and a bunch of rabbits. Solar panels on the roof of his house and barn are hooked to two large battery banks with inverters for power. Rain barrels feeding into larger tanks in a few places. Wood stove inside. I laughed – he even has a working outhouse though he said they really don't use it.

As Ben and I talked we found that we thought a lot a like. He expressed concern about the economy and the world today. He talked about trying to set up his family to be as independent from the rest of the world as possible. Awesome. I agreed with most all of his opinions – but I really didn't talk about preparedness. Maybe another day.

- Jed

June 24th   A day of relaxation.......

Restful day today. Got up and went to church for early service. Cleaned my guns from shooting with Ben. Picked some cucumbers and still have some lettuce growing. Love homemade salad. Watched a couple of DVD's and just caught up on some reading.

Need to check out a couple of the preparedness caches that I buried to make sure they are remaining waterproof. I dread digging down that deep just to fill it back in – but need to do it. Burying survival supplies.....my brother thinks I am nuts. I think I might start writing down lists in this journal – things to do, things to get, etc.

Thought about "M" a bit today. Really wish I had just forgotten about her like I am sure she did with me. The reality is 20 years ago I fell in love with her and never fell out. The Reunion is in a week. Going to be interesting.

- Jed

June 25th   Is the "trigger" about to be pulled?.......

Man – HUGE news today and scary.

Yesterday a container in the Charleston harbor was found to contain a small nuclear weapon. The government is being hush-hush about it as the news was apparently leaked and not supposed to go public. I am very nervous now and I am not alone. Many preparedness websites are putting a call out to all preppers to make their final preparations as they feel "something" is getting ready to happen.

The President made a supportive statement stating that the finding of a "weapon of mass destruction" in Charleston shows that the many law enforcement agencies involved have the safety and security of the United

States under control. I wonder if he has ever taken a look at the country's southern border.

I think I am going to make another withdrawal from the bank. Would rather have food in the cabinet and ammo in my rifle if the SHTF than cash in the bank.

Going to have trouble getting to sleep.

- Jed

June 26th   Taking time off from work.......

Took the rest of the week off from work – used vacation time. Spent much of today working in the garden and organizing my prep's. Eric did a couple of raised beds and I gave him all of the profit. He went and opened a savings account which hopefully is a sign of positive things to come from him. Went and bought several additional totes and started separating items such as cooking, first aid, tools, winter supplies, etc. Labeled everything for easy identification.

Always been concerned that if the SHTF how would my community make it or would I be on my own. I know a few of the neighbors – some better than others:

- Mark and Jessica live across the street. They are not preppers in any way and have a little 5 year old girl. Good people. I am good friends with Mark.
- Jillian and Ryan live up the street. Do not know them very well but I know Ryan was in the military.
- Bill and Kerri seem to be good people. Have gone over to their house a few times on cookouts. Bill is a correctional officer at the local Justice Center and is familiar with firearms. I also know he

has some martial arts experience. They also have two teenage daughters.

- Paul and Michelle are a few doors down and have a nice garden every year. Michelle is a teacher.
- Next door neighbors Thomas and Charlene are quiet and independent people. I talk to Thomas once in a while. He grew up in the country and hunts often and has had a garden almost every year.
- Mike and Jennifer live on the other side of the neighborhood. I used to work with Mike years ago at the local airport. They have six kids and a lot of family in the area.

That's about it. Trying to be totally on my own I do not think is realistic.

- Jed

June 27th   *Things are heating up.......*

Enjoying my time off from work, however, spent most of the day in front of the TV watching Fox News after a few errands this morning.

There was some kind of chemical spill along the Mexican border between the city of Nuevo Laredo in Mexico and Laredo Texas. News is somewhat sketchy however several miles along the border have been evacuated. Many people were killed and sickened as whatever was released was carried by the wind – apparently. Details are few. There are rumors that a terrorist cell was trying to smuggle some chemical/biological agent into the United States and something went wrong. With what is going on in the rest of the world along with the Charleston nuke finding – enough to make the hairs on the back of my neck stand up.

At lunch time I went for a ride on my mountain bike on a few light trails – great exercise. Spent a lot of money on the bike but just do not ride often enough. I did have in the back of my mind that it would be a good secondary "survival" vehicle.

Talked to Diane on the phone for awhile. She said she wanted us to take a weekend trip WITH THE KIDS. I have met them but she is very protective, which I understand. This is a good sign for "us".

As for the errands this morning – picked up a few supplies:

- Several tarps of different sizes at Northern Tools
- Bought 500 rounds of .223 PMC at Nichol's Store. They are usually on the expensive side but they had a special sale going on.
- 20 gallons of spring water in jugs
- Extra set of FRS/GMRS radio's
- 5 gallons of Clorox bleach
- 4 large cases of toilet paper
- Picked up a local map of Rock Hill, York, and Chester
- Filled up all of my propane tanks
- 100 packs of various vegetable seeds from the Dollar Store – price was 10 for $1.00. Eric gives these to customers of his raised bed gardening business.

UPS delivered some spare magazines I ordered from Brownell's.

- *Jed*

June 28th   No solutions.......

I am enjoying writing in this "diary". Started it to clear my head as well as document my thoughts and feelings. Maybe I will be able pass this on to what I hope is my future family.

The way I see the government handling the economy and the national deficit.....I do not see any good solution to it all. The debt continues to grow and the economy is like a slug – barely moving forward. I see serious problems in the future. It is just a matter of <u>when</u>. Society seems to be breaking up as massive groups of people are so far on opposite sides of opinions "United We Stand" seems like a very distant memory. Politics are full of power hungry millionaires that have interests in themselves and how they can get more money and more power. It's a shame this country is spiraling downward as quickly as it is.

Glad to have the preps I have. People still think I am nuts for storing extra food, water, and firearms. Having bug out bags, get home bags, hidden caches, etc. may go totally to waste. That is fine by me. With some of the recent events I swear I can smell it in the air that something bad is going to happen.

Well – if it all goes to waste I will leave a lot of toilet paper to someone. Every time they "go" ......they will think of me.

- Jed

June 29th   A bad dream and a funny movie.......

Had a dream last night – a nightmare more like it. You know how dreams are – not exactly sure how it happened but basically the SHTF. Economy failed? Not sure. All I know is the country had fallen apart and people were on their own. Lawlessness all over. Waves of crime engulfed large areas. I remember in my dream that the military had mostly dissolved as soldiers went to be with their families. Police officers did the same as they were vastly understaffed to deal with the situation. Hospitals were overrun early on. Power was out pretty much across the country. Desperation.

I woke up and immediately watched *Ferris Bueller's Day Off* – one of my favorite comedies. Just wanted to lighten the day after that dream. After the movie went to SAM's and shopped for more food and some misc supplies. On the way home I stopped at Nichol's Gun Shop and grabbed some extra magazines for my S&W M&P15-22 – one of my favorite plinkers. Also went to Wal-Mart and bought most of their supply of 9mm and CCI Mini-Mag .22LR ammo.

I feel pretty decent about my preps. I am still a long way off from where I would eventually like to be – but I have come along way.

Hardly thought about the reunion tomorrow which is a good thing because my stomach has been in knots about it? Still thinking about "M". Why am I so nervous? Here I am this survivalist with all these guns, martial arts training and I am super nervous to see ....*the person I had hoped to spend the rest of my life with. Ugh!!*

Diane met me for lunch as she is flying out tomorrow to see her parents in Washington, DC. We held hands during lunch and she confided that she has enjoyed the time we have spent together. We decided to take a trip up to the mountains in two weeks. The kids are staying in Washington for a month. Looks to be a good trip for just the two of us.

Will be heading out in the morning for Athens to the reunion.

- Jed

June 30th   The reunion arrives.......

Today was nerve racking as well as exciting.

The reunion in Athens was not until 5:00pm so I ran a few errands prior to heading out. Eric and I ran to Lowe's and picked up the supplies for installation of a couple of raised beds for clients. The cost of the wood went up again so we may have to increase the price a bit. Eric and I had a good talk while driving about responsibility and the future. These last several days he seems to be getting it. I don't know. Reminded him I was heading to Georgia shortly and to make sure he keeps the house locked up as well as the gates to the fence in the backyard.

I already had the Jeep packed up last night and headed out at 12:00 noon. The Jeep was great and the weather perfect as I drove the back route (Hwy 72) most of the way. While driving I listened to some AM radio when I could get it and there was a confirmation that the "incident" in Mexico along the boarder was some type of chemical situation. Apparently a terrorist cell was trying to smuggle in some type of chemical weapon and something went wrong and the "device" was detonated. Of course everyone is asking questions – *"How do we know this is the only one? How do we know that other groups didn't make it across?"*

I made it to Athens on time, checked into the hotel and made it downstairs to the large Conference Room for the Reunion at 5:00pm. I ran into a couple friends from school right off including Mitch and Gary. They are buddies I hung out with back in school. I needed to go to the bathroom and just as I passed by the Women's Restroom the door flung open and hit me in the shoulder. I said instinctively, "Excuse me." It was then I realized that the person standing right in front of me was M.

M was right in front of me. She was older but the same. She smiled at me and said "Hi". We made some small talk about where we were living, told her she looked great, asked her if she had kids (no) and she asked me back. The tension was thick in the air as I wanted to ask her if she was married but resisted. She asked instead and I quickly – probably too quickly answered no. She then mentioned she just got divorced a few month ago. I lied and told her I was sorry to hear that. I still had to go to the bathroom but I suffered through.

The rest of the night we talked about jobs, hobbies, friends we knew, school, etc. It was really great. We were both staying in the same hotel as the Reunion and decided to meet the next morning for breakfast. She told me she was glad I came to the Reunion.

Wow! I can't wait until tomorrow. Not sure how I will ever get to sleep.

- Jed

July 1st   It happened.......

I am not even sure what to say at this point. Today the United States came under attack and I do not think this country will ever be the same.

I woke up this morning around 4:00am hearing screaming and yelling and found the power was out. To sum it up so I can get to sleep – several nuclear bombs went off across the United States – from what I hear. I say that because communication is pretty limited. Some of the people I ran into in the hallways at the hotel told me what they heard over the radio and on TV prior to losing power. With all of what has happened within the last two weeks I guess the writing was on the wall.

I am worried about radiation. I don't know where all the attacks happened. The only city I heard mentioned at first was Chicago. As I was leaving Athens I was glad the Reunion was not held in the center of the city. Even on the outer edges people were panicking. I saw a Wal-Mart parking lot packed full of cars and a line at the door. There were police cars in the parking lot with their lights flashing. I am not sure how they are paying for food with the power out. Hope they have cash.

I have got to try to get some sleep. It is 1:00am and....oh, a major thing I guess I have left out – M is with me. After I found out what happened I went to her room. She flew to the Reunion from Arizona where her home is. I told her what happened and after we talked a bit I told her she needed to come with me as I traveled back home. I told her likely there would be no flying for a few weeks - just like after 9/11. In my mind I truly felt there may be no flying for months. Convinced her that she could take a flight out of Charlotte when they start back up. M didn't want to be left alone in that hotel.

I had a set of maps and programmed my GPS to drive some back roads rather than try to drive up Interstate 85. Travel was still slow and I had to take some long routes to get where we are now. We drove 8 hours and are almost halfway home. I did get more news on the radio during the drive -

Cities hit with nukes that I know of so far:

- Boston

- Chicago

- Denver

- Washington, DC

- Baltimore

- Norfolk

- San Diego

What about Diane and the kids?

That is so far. There were also reported attacks on dams and electrical power plants across the country. A lot of news is sketchy. Hope to learn more tomorrow – I just want to get home. Eric is probably freaking out. It is very strange not being able to make a simple cell phone call.

We stopped in Greenwood and I found a small rundown hotel that was accepting cash. Also found a gas station open and was able to refill the tank. My spare tank of 5 gallons is still available if I need it. I am glad I had $500 stashed in the back under one of the rear seats. I took the floor while M has the bed. She is scared for her brother who works in New York City. She was also very nervous as I brought my M&P9 into the hotel room.

We held hands a bit before saying good night and I tried to comfort her by saying that I would keep her safe.

Things are going to get bad quickly I suspect. I have tried to mentally prepare myself for something like this. M is another story. I have my phone -which has no signal anymore – set to wake us up in 3 hours so we can get back on the road.

- Jed

July 2nd   Made it home.......

Finally got home at 2:00pm today. Eric was OK. Along the entire trip most all areas were without power but not all. Was able to get some news on the radio.

- Most people are calling in sick for all jobs. With the power out many businesses are closed anyway. People are staying home to be with their families.
- The attack is a little over 24 hours old and crime is spreading already. On the radio they said stores were wiped out of food,

water and other essentials. People are panicking and police are being called to deal with violent and unhappy customers.

- There are reported shootings and rapes throughout the country. Low-life's are taking advantage of law enforcement getting spread so thin. I wonder how bad it is already in the big cities that have survived.

- Radio is reporting that the government – or what is left of it – is instituting curfews throughout.....South Carolina at least. Not sure of the rest of the country. Citizens must be off the streets from dusk till dawn. They are trying to get control over the lawlessness.

- Still more talk of some other non-nuclear attacks including chemical weapons. Nothing specific.

M is doing OK. We talked a lot on the road. We finally talked about "us" and what happened after graduation. Turns out she always wondered the same thing I did – *"What happened?"* Bottom line is we were just kids. I could tell through all the turmoil and stress that there was still a connection. We discussed preparedness and she felt reassured when I told her about my preps.

Eric did a good job with the house while I was away. He had loaded up a Remington 870 Tactical shotgun and stood guard watching the front and back. He was scared.

I have got to get some sleep. I am going to pray for this country and all those innocent people killed yesterday and those that are struggling to survive. How many thousands have died? It's difficult to comprehend.

- Jed

July 3rd   Community, concern and more news.......

Woke up this morning thinking that I have got to get organized. I suspect the power will be out for a long time, running water may not last, the supplies we have we need to make last.

Sunlight lit most of the house and flashlights were used elsewhere. I got with M and Eric and had a good talk with them. For 15 minutes I talked about how fragile our countries internal supply system is and it is likely stores, once closed, would not be resupplied nor reopen for many months. We also discussed crime and what WROL is (Without Rule of Law). I explained that life was going to be very different moving forward and we needed to start getting ready. M started crying when she realized her chances of getting home were slim. I told her she had a place to stay as long as she wanted.

I asked Eric and M if they could check the garden and pick what was ready. I also asked if they could start inventorying EVERYTHING in the house and garage so we can see what we have. I am thinking down the road about barter. I wanted to go over to see Mark and Jessie.

Mark and Jessie were OK. I gave them some tips on food storage and rationing as well as talked about trying to stay strong for their 5 year old daughter – Addie. I asked Mark if they had a gun in the house and they didn't. I asked him to come over around 9:30pm tonight (when it is dark). He did and I gave him a Smith & Wesson 22A .22LR pistol. I went over the controls, explained safety rules, and watched him change the magazine out a couple times and release the slide. I gave him the pistol along with 4 10-rd magazines and 300 rounds of CCI Blazer .22LR. Mark has been a good friend and they are good people. By the way – Jessie is absolutely anti-gun. I suspect her mind will be changing.

I talked to Bill up the road. He was still reporting to the Moss Justice Center (jail) daily. He said many of his fellow Correctional Officers were not reporting to work. He was able to refuel his vehicle at the city yard along with the Police. He also has been hearing from city and county officers that crime was getting bad. It's only been a few days. I have to start putting some better security plans in effect. I need to talk to more people in neighborhood tomorrow.

I am going to stay up until 3:00am keeping an eye on things. Moon is pretty bright.....luckily.

 - Jed

July 4th   Independence Day.......

This day has been an emotional one for myself and many others. As a day that often has been celebrated with cookouts and friends/families getting together - THIS Independence Day was different.

The reality of what has happened is sinking in to many. Just a few days without power and modern comforts is literally putting folks on the brink of suicide. Years of instant "everything" – food, water, hot showers, entertainment, air conditioning – has led to incredible stress on those not prepared. Now it is taking a lot of effort and preparation just to cook a small meal. There is no TV, DVD's, no drive-thru's to get a "Happy Meal". It is summertime here in the South and the heat is relentless with no air conditioning. With the heat – water is even more critical.

I got with Eric and M today regarding defense. We have the shotgun at the front door. I am carrying my S&W M&P 9mm on my side constantly. My Stag AR stays with e when I am on watch at night. I told them I feel like we need to set up "watch rotations" to monitor activity around the house. It is just a matter of time before some desperate folks make their way through the neighborhood.

We are all watching everything during daylight hours. From 9:00pm until 1:00am Eric is on watch. From 1:00 until 4:00am it is me and from 4:00 till 8:00 M is on watch. I have small trip alarms set up along the entire length of the fence in the backyard. If anything tries to climb over the fence – a loud shrieking alarm will sound. These were a great deal as the main "trip" was bought at the local Dollar Store for $1.00 each. I will set these up out front as well.

Tomorrow I am going door to door to try to set up a neighborhood meeting about what has happened.

 - Jed

July 5th   Will we unite?

Problem: We are running out of clean clothes and that is one part of my preps I never considered. I can only turn my underwear inside out so many times. OK, that was a joke. :-)

I spent several hours going to door to door asking everyone if they would go to the model home in the neighborhood tonight at 5:00pm to discuss what is happening. A few people asked for details and I just said I thought it would be good to get together and discuss news and how everyone is doing. I did find quite a few homes with no one home as I rode my bike around.

Most of the neighborhood showed up and I asked for everyone's attention. I had an agenda with some discussion ideas wrote down. Everyone was pretty accepting of me. Most everyone was scared and looking at the future with a lot of uncertainty.

We discussed the following:

- o   Reality of the Situation

- o Status of Your Supplies – food, water, medicine
- o Sanitation
- o Defense/Security
- o Gardens & Rainwater Capture
- o Next Meeting

I have never been good in front of a crowd but I think I did well. I spelled out the seriousness of the situation and tried to get across to everyone that if we worked together we would all benefit, and stand a better chance to survive. I also told everyone they had very little time left if they wanted to start a garden. Some people had seeds and with Eric's raised bed business we had some extra supplies which could help. I also mentioned that everyone needed to be prepared to capture rain.

Of the 30 people that showed up many asked questions and gave their opinion on topics. A few asked about the government helping, and when the mail would start back up. I had to disappoint them with my answer.

Lastly – we decided to all go home and sleep on what was discussed – and meet the next day at 2:00pm at the model house.

M told me she was proud of me – that I looked like I actually knew what I was talking about. I thanked her. We sat outside enjoying the cooler temperature of the night and talked. I told her that although I wished none of this had ever happened – I was glad she was here. She just smiled – but I could tell she was unsettled. It has got to be tough for her – in a strange place surrounded by strange people.

Need to get some sleep before it is my turn to go on watch detail.

- Jed

July 6th   Terror in the night.......

Mark came over and woke me up this morning just as the sun was coming up. Something happened on the other side of the neighborhood nearest the utility road. An old couple – Mr. and Mrs. Greenfield, were robbed and killed last night. Someone heard a couple gunshots around 2:00am - and watched out their window. They saw someone about 10 minutes later leaving the Greenfield's house using a flashlight.

I asked Mark if the neighbor that heard the shooting did anything. The answer was "No". They were scared for their own life and didn't want to get involved. Once the sun started peeking over the horizon another neighbor went to the house and discovered the bodies.

We had our second meeting and more of the neighborhood showed up. Concern about safety was growing especially after word of the Greenfield's spread through the neighborhood. I led the meeting with a prayer for the Greenfield's.

After the prayer we discussed some the same agenda items as yesterday:

- Defense/Security
- Gardens & Rainwater Capture
- Next Meeting

Defense & Security – I told everyone that I thought it would be a good idea to start a "neighborhood watch". Everyone agreed. With the number of people to pull from we should be able cover the perimeter pretty decent. Ryan – Jillian's husband – said he was in the military and would help organize the patrol's. Volunteers were asked for and the 16-17 people that raised there hands agreed to meet at 5:00pm.

Gardens and Rainwater Capture – I really emphasized the point that it is imperative that EVERYONE work to plant gardens to supplement their food supply. Many expressed frustration not only with their lack of knowledge on what to do and lack of equipment – but also with the effort that needed to be put forth. I was shocked as we are talking about their lives. It still hasn't sunk in yet with some of them. I agreed to have a gardening class the next morning and provide some seeds to those that needed them from Eric's raised bed supplies.

We agreed to meet again the next day at 2:00pm.

Prior to ending the meeting I left something for everyone to think about. I told them that although they might think things are bad – it is going to get much, much worse. The Greenfield's are just a sign of things to come and if **our** community does not come together in a big way - our chances will not be good.

M and I worked on washing some clothes. Basically we used three 5 gallon buckets of water. First bucket had soapy water in it, second was clean water, and third was a final clean rinse water. Once we were done the clothes were hung to dry. Another technique we are trying is just hanging some shirts up without getting them wet first to see of the suns rays will sanitize them. Water is valuable so we used all the grey water in the garden – except the first bucket.

M, Eric, and I are splitting up chores and working well together. Eric is doing great – I am proud of him.

Need to get some sleep.

- Jed

July 7th   M and I get closer.......

The community met once again and close to 45 people were there. Things are coming together - albeit on the slow side. I made more suggestions including forming teams to try to get certain things done and to take advantage of peoples skill sets.

Right now the teams include:

- Security
- Gardening
- Water
- Medical
- Communication
- and Kid's

The Kid's Team was brought up by Jessie – Mark's wife. She is a teacher and said many of the kids are very sad, withdrawn, and depressed. No kidding. All these kids are used to computers, smartphones, and of course TV – all of which are pretty much gone. The Kid's Team will get the kids together and play games, color, and try to have fun. What a great idea.

Ryan briefed everyone on the patrol schedule and noted that all patrol members would have a colored ribbon on their left arm so they could be identified. There were three shifts right now and each shift changed colors daily.

Everyone wants me to be a member of their team. I decided to assist wherever I could but my concentration was with Security and Gardening. Eric also joined the Gardening Team.

More later on that stuff.

M and I are getting closer. We are living under the same roof. We take turns in the solar shower. I know she has caught me staring at her. I can't help it. I think there is something between us and it is not distant memories – something new. I just came out and asked her while we were finishing a couple glasses of wine what was happening between us. She got up out of her chair and kissed me on the cheek, and looked into my eyes, and told me that she has never stopped caring. She then went inside and went to bed.

The world around me is in complete turmoil and somehow I can't help but feel happiness inside with M with me. Am I selfish?

Maybe.

- Jed

July 8th   News from the outside.......

Due to the crime, and no reason really to go anywhere plus needing to conserve gas – I haven't left the neighborhood in over a week. From what I hear a couple people from the neighborhood have ventured out and never returned. I took the Jeep along with Bill - the correctional officer and fellow Security Team member – for a short jaunt. So strange and terrifying as well. There were literally no cars on the road and saw very few people walking around. We saw several bodies lying in yards and on the streets baking in the sun. We drove up next to one and the stench almost made me puke let alone the open cavity in the back of this poor souls head. No doubt violence is taking over.

Stores were closed – all of them. Every storefront we drove past had all the windows broken out. No gas – no stores – no vehicles. It was like a movie where everyone just disappears. The extreme heat of the southern sun as well as the danger is likely keeping people indoors. Temperature reached 102 today.

Just in case of trouble Bill had a Mossberg 500 with a **Choate** pistol grip stock at the ready. 00-Buck filled the tube and the chamber. Between the seats my Stag M4 sat. I was wearing a Maxpedition Mini Tactical Vest stuffed with three **30-rd Magpul magazines**. My M&P 9mm pistol sat in a holster which I mounted under the steering column.

We ran across a guy walking down the main street – looked out of place. We watched him for awhile and decided to approach. We pulled up and he jumped and started to run. We yelled to him that it was OK and he slowed down and looked at us. Bill stuck a bottle of water and a jar of peanut butter out the window of the Jeep. He walked over – Bill had his left fist wrapped around the grip of his Mossberg. The guy – his name was.....yup, you guessed it...."Guy". We asked what was going on and where everyone was. He replied that a lot of his neighbors left. He went on to say that many went to stay with relatives that lived in the country. He also said that he knew of some that killed themselves – and others that were victims of criminals..... permanently. He said that in the bad sections of town mass murders happened as those not unfamiliar with breaking the law started taking what they needed. Guy continued that groups of young immoral men would bust into a house and kill a whole family – expect for the young girls. They would take any supplies they found as well as the girls. He didn't need to tell us what the girls were for. He also said he has not seen a police car in days. We wished him luck, gave him the water and peanut butter, and drove on.

The ride home Bill and I didn't say a word to each other. We didn't need to. We drove down the road....angry.

Bill and I returned and got with the rest of the Security Team and informed them about the trip. We are certainly not alone but from the drive we gathered that most everyone that is still around is staying inside – and that security has got to become the primary focus of the community.

There are very few radio stations broadcasting. Tonight we were able to pick up some additional information from stations we have not been able to get before.

- 12 seems to be the correct number of nuclear weapons that went off across the United States.

- Boston

- Chicago

- Denver

- Washington, DC

- Baltimore

- Norfolk

- San Diego

- San Francisco

- Houston

- Indianapolis

- Miami

- Philadelphia

- Numerous other targets were hit with chemical/biological weapons.
- As soon as the attack occurred all domestic nuclear power plants went into shutdown mode – preventing additional disaster.
- Several dams were hit and flood water released killing countless thousands.
- A few major electrical plants were also destroyed.
- England apparently was also attacked.
- The state of the population is extremely desperate.
- The government has been rendered powerless. Mostly state governments are making the minimal efforts. People are pretty much on their own.
- Just as we lost the station we heard something about US military at war overseas – but with whom?

Details remain pretty sketchy. One question everyone is wondering is who is responsible. I certainly would like to know but it will not change the situation. If we are going to make it this community has to work together as a team.

It's been one week since The Event. I am going to try to get EVERYONE in the neighborhood together tomorrow to see exactly where we are at with our efforts.

 - Jed

July 9th   A plan is set.......

I walked the entire neighborhood knocking on doors and asked people to attend the meeting at the model house at 5:00pm. Most all said they would attend. 110 houses in the neighborhood, 12 were empty prior to The Event from foreclosure, 16 more I had no answer at the door, and looks like no one home. That leaves 82 occupied homes.

Close to 80 people showed up at the meeting. This one was interesting as when I started talking about my agenda someone stood up that I did not know and asked who elected me leader. I asked him his name – which he answered, "Neil". I told Neil that no one elected me leader and I do not proclaim myself to be the leader of the community. I went on to say that before The Event happened I was what some people would call a "survivalist" or a "prepper" and had started to prepare for troubled times. Although I always hoped that nothing significant would happen – I have done a decent amount of research and put a lot of thought into the "what if?" I continued to tell him that I am here to help others as well as myself get through what is going to be an extremely difficult situation and that we needed to work together.

I asked Neil if he had any other questions and he answered, rather suspiciously, *"Not right now...."*

I talked to the group summarizing what had been done thus far. I talked about the Security, Gardening, Water, Medical, Communication, and Kid's Team.

- I talked about the trip that Bill and I went on and some of the details. There were kids around so I did not want to get too graphic.
- I talked about the need for more volunteers with the Security patrols. Ryan discussed the current rotations and what he wanted to be able to do. He was Military Police National Guard out of Florence, SC for a few years after regular duty in the Army. He also served in Iraq several years ago. People responded to him well. Ryan brought up we need to secure the perimeter better as well as set up some method of looking over the neighborhood better – visually.
- I expressed the absolute need to get seeds in the ground and to can any extra produce that anyone has from their garden. We could not afford to let anything go to waste. I mentioned that Eric was with the Gardening Team and to see him for information and help.

- The water stopped flowing a few days ago from the city. I mentioned about catching rain water as well as setting up a water detail to gather water from the local "swamp" and filter it. The Water Team would build several large water filters from plans I had (LDS manual). A few people had small kiddy pools that were full which was great. I recommended that a rotation get set up so everyone can do their fair share in toting the water.

At this point Neil stood up and yelled that he had heard enough. He went on to say that I should not be making decisions for him or anyone else. He stormed off. I was relieved when several in the group stood up and said that Neil did not speak for the rest of the group. They said that they appreciated the advice and help and wanted me to continue to lead the meetings. The rest of the 80 or so people clapped. Wow!

At that point I told everyone that tomorrow would be a great day to start getting the community moving forward. I had all the Team members come to the front and I asked everyone else to select a team they would like to help out with and meet with them.

Security Leader – Ryan

Gardening – Eric

Water – Phillip

Medical – Rose

Communication – Bill

Kids – Jessie

After all the Team Leaders got with the volunteers I met with the leaders to discuss their goals and objectives.

I am happy with the direction things are going however I do not think that most understand how difficult.....and dangerous things are going to get.

- Jed

July 10th   Moving along.......

I was impressed with the efforts of everyone in the community today. One of the water filters was built via instructions in my LDS Preparedness Manual. Folks are transporting water and filtering it. The Security Team got together with volunteers and put together a better patrol schedule using 8 people per shift plus he managed to set up communications between everyone. Eric worked with 40 houses to assist in building raised beds and till lawns for gardens. Several folks already had gardens and donated some seeds along with what Eric had. An offshoot of the Gardening Team decided to go on a hunt for rabbits, squirrels and anything else that could be found. Everything looks to be moving along including the Kid's Team which gathered many kids in the neighborhood and played a few games and even had some Kool-Aid (I knew I stocked up on that Kool-Aid powder for a reason).

I can't help but feel uneasy as things seem to be coming together too easy. I noticed Neil was nowhere to be seen. Add to that two guys on motorcycles drove right through the neighborhood today. They did not stop and they did not say anything. This shows just how vulnerable we are. I am going to get with Ryan about this.

I need to get with Bill on communications. I have been so busy I am not sure what is happening with that – especially with no power. I wish I had bought a shortwave radio or a HAM before. It was always on my list of things to do.

M and I had dinner together by candlelight (as usual). Beef Stew over a bed of rice with a little bread that M made today from some "*add water only*" mix I stashed away. A little wine made the evening seem almost normal. We made small talk for awhile and then she asked about her chances of making it home. I asked her if she wanted me to be honest and she said yes. I told her I did not think there was any chance for a long, long time. She began to cry a bit and I moved my chair over to hers and put my arm around her. She looked up at me and said she wanted to stay with me. I told her as long as she wanted to. At that point she looked up at me and we just looked into each others eyes. It was one of those rare, miraculous moments when two human beings connect on a level that just cannot be put into words. I leaned in and we kissed.

I am glad I had that wine.

- Jed

July 11th   Getting ready for visitors.......

The seeds are spouting in many of the gardens. Everyone is realizing that although there are no typical jobs to drive to each day there is a lot of work to be done. Those working their garden have to pick insects off the plants, weed and water. These gardens are no longer just a hobby but an integral part of their survival.

I met with Ryan and Bill today and talked about the motorcycle's that went through the neighborhood yesterday. We discussed that the neighborhood is far too open. Those motorcycle riders were likely feeling us out. The Security Team decided to barricade the entrance-way, including the driveway along with all areas on either side. The goal is to prevent any vehicle from entering the entrance. Luckily there had been a couple of partial builds in the neighborhood which afforded us quite a bit of lumber, nails and concrete. Several trash can were filled with dirt and spaced out across the entire entrance. A fence was built with the 2×4's as well. Security also placed a pair of members patrolling the entrance at all times.

Great find today – one of the neighbor's, Ted, brought forward a scanner. He had not thought of it early on because of no power. I took the scanner to Bill's along with one of my solar panels, inverters, and a charge controller to power it. Bill already had a small set up with AM/FM and a CB. With the solar panel he can run everything more frequently. Hopefully we will have some more news tomorrow due to the scanner.

I am so tired. I am more physically active than I ever have been. There is constantly something that needs to be done. My body ache's and my muscles are sore. M gave me a great massage tonight when it cooled down. A small piece of paradise it was!!

The community is going to be tested soon. I can feel it. We need to be ready and we have a long way to go.

- Jed

July 12th   A world in turmoil.......

Next to the night The Event happened, I have never felt so uneasy. The scanner Ted gave us brought forth news that is both incredible and terrifying all at once.

Here is what we have so far:

- United States military forces are at war overseas. The United States nuked Iran and North Korea. They apparently were largely responsible for the attack on the United States. Forces are patrolling and continue to engage these two countries. Other Muslim countries such as Pakistan have taken up for Iran and are getting involved.

- Most all domestic military forces have disbanded and returned home to their families.
- Canada, Israel, and England are on our side. Israel and England are dealing with some of their own issues as well and apparently assisted in the attack on Iran.
- Germany is staying independent and says they are sitting this one out.
- I am not sure the exact reason – but the United States right after The Event nuked China. China returned with a very limited response and all of their nuclear missiles were brought down prior reaching the United States. China went from over a billion people to less than 500 million from the estimates given. I am guessing China was targeted for a reason?
- Cities across the United States are in absolute chaos. Massive amounts of crime, little to no law enforcement response, murder, rapes, and kidnappings - terrible. Apparently we are very lucky to have made it thus far so "easy". People have no food, no water. Medical facilities have been overwhelmed; especially those anywhere near the nuclear sites. Desperation is traveling across the United States like a tidal wave.
- It is reported that radiation danger is minimal and mostly localized to the denotation cities.

If the people in this community need something else to motivate them – this should be it.

- Jed

July 13th   Community is threatened.......

As if the news last night wouldn't be enough to darken the day – a group of people came to the front gate asking for food and water.

The group consisted of 8 men and women. The Security Team members radioed Ryan who then radioed Bill and I. We went to the gate and within the few minutes it took us to get there the small crowd started getting upset.

I talked to Ryan and Bill and addressed the issue of charity. I told them if we give them anything not only will they likely return for more, but others will no doubt hear of it and more will come. Bill and Ryan said they didn't see anything wrong with giving them water. I voted against it. I know it may seem cruel – but I felt that it's what had to be done.

Several gallons of water were provided to the 8 people – who after taking it asked about the food. Ryan stood up and told them water was all we could afford to give. A couple of the men started yelling that they were starving and their wives needed food. Ryan looked at me and I said no shaking my head. Ryan relayed the answer to the group. At that point one of the men pulled out pistol from his pocket. Ryan, two members of the Security patrol, and me drew on the man quickly. The guy's wife jumped in front of him and pushed the gun down. We told the group to move on immediately.

They complied and were not happy. We didn't even get a thank you for the water.

I talked to Bill and Ryan after group was long gone and emphasized my disagreement with giving away our supplies. They both said that they tended to agree with me after thinking a bit – but it was too late. This encounter could have turned a lot worse if the group had been better armed and organized.

- Jed

July 14th   Wishing life was normal.......

Woke up today feeling rather depressed – even with M with me.

I miss "normal" life. Going to the grocery store to pick up a gallon of milk. Running through the drive-thru at Burger King for a quick burger. Watching a great movie at the movie theater. How about air conditioning!?! Picking up the phone and calling a friend. Would have been nice to be attending a preparedness conference today rather than living the life I had prepared for – but hoped wouldn't happen.

Everything is so difficult and slow. Preparing meals takes much more time and preparation. It was 88 degrees today and cooking over an open flame – HOT!! Sick of the heat and I would like to wish for the Fall and Winter but then the opposite problem will happen – the cold will come. I haven't been thinking about that but need to.

I am alive and our situation is somewhat stable. I am lucky to have the food stores I have put away. I wonder how Ben is doing. He is not far but with the streets as dangerous as they are – it is not a good drive to make. Maybe tomorrow I will see if Bill – or maybe even M – would like to take the drive and see how he is doing.

Oh, I had Mark and Jessie bring me over one of those little portable DVD players with the built in screen and battery. I charged it using my solar system. That allowed their little girl, Addie, to watch a Disney movie for a couple hours. I bet she had a new appreciation for such a treat.

Gotta get some sleep.

- Jed

July 15th   Trip to Ben's.......

Rained today – which was great. My rain barrels filled back up and many in the neighborhood were able to gather some rain via different methods. Some used kiddie pools, some used upside down umbrella's and soda bottles, buckets, etc. This will be a big help to all those that have just started their gardens. Rainwater seems to just do the trick for a struggling garden.

I took M over to Ben's today. Great trip for the community. We drove the Jeep over and it was mostly uneventful. As usual back roads were driven and I did not see very many people. We did see a few houses that were burnt down and also lots of evidence of vandalism – cars with broken windows and graffiti on buildings. Some of the graffiti consisted of racial words sprayed on the sides of a couple houses. Pathetic.

When we arrived to Ben's his front gate and property had signs that read "IF YOU CAN READ THIS SIGN YOU ARE ALREADY IN RANGE!" I wondered if I should even attempt to contact him. The front gate was locked so I walked up his driveway while M waited in the Jeep ready to drive off if things went bad. I left my AR in the Jeep with M and walked with my Smith & Wesson M&P 9mm on my hip. Ben came out of his single floor cabin-looking house and met me with a handshake.

We were very glad to see each other and he said he had been wondering how I was doing. I filled him in on the community and the challenges we had moving forward (food, water, and security). He filled me in on what has been going on around his property:

- o **His son Jeff and family had made their way to Ben's place**. Jeff is an excellent metal fabricator and welder.
- o **Ben's nephew Jeremiah also made it to Ben's place**. Jeremiah spent 6 years in the military including 2 tours in Iraq.
- o **Ben's best friend – Matt, and family also took residence on Ben's farm**. Ben and Matt grew up together.

Ben told me that they have had some violent encounters since The Event. On two occasions people have tried to sneak in and steal food out of the gardens or steal eggs from the chicken coupes. The first encounter resulted in the person getting run off – scared. The second did not go so well. Ben had to shoot the trespasser after the man pulled a pistol. He said he felt horrible about it but he had to do it.

We ate a good mid-afternoon meal of fresh eggs and some bread and butter. Talking about how good the fresh eggs were and how the freeze dried eggs and bacon we had been eating just wasn't a comparison – Ben made us an offer. He offered up some chickens for the community in exchange for some help building a small shelter for storing firewood. I could tell he was really just helping us out – charity.

Of course I accepted. We agreed to come the next day to help and when we were done we would bring the chickens back. When M and I got back to the neighborhood I talked to Eric about the chickens. He is going to get with the Gardening Team and build a chicken coop tomorrow.

I love eggs.

- Jed

July 16th The garden, more news, and squirrels gone.......

My generator was fired up for the first time since The Event. Eric hauled it over to where the chicken coops were being built – two of them. Ben ended up giving us six hens – which made us very happy. We got one rooster – which may make the hens happy. He has many more and we anticipate taking some of the eggs and allowing them to hatch. With six hens we should get 4 eggs or so per day. Two eggs each will be given to two households. It's not much but more than we had.

If we can get some more hens from the eggs – in a few months our egg output will increase dramatically.

The squirrels around the neighborhood have dried up. They are just not being seen much anymore. I imagine that in the past couple weeks most of them have been shot and eaten. Rabbits were never seen very much and still have to be hunted. I placed some snares out around the perimeter of the neighborhood but so far nothing.

Bill updated us on some news he heard over the scanner. Apparently in California there is some kind of sickness spreading. Not a lot of details other than symptoms include high fever, severe vomiting, diarrhea, and eventual death. The body just shuts down. It's on the other side of the country but I am still concerned. With the limited movement of people now – especially with no planes – it should take quite some time for it to reach the east coast if it ever does.

Interesting the variety of firearms the people on Security Patrol are carrying. There are a couple of AR's, couple of Mini-14's, a Remington 7600 .30-06, several Ruger 10/22's, an old Marlin Camp 9, one AK-47, some Mossberg and Remington shotguns, and a few bolt actions. Pistols of all sizes and shapes. One of the problems is there are so many types of guns and calibers that ammunition can't be shared nor magazines. At least we have a decent number of armed patrols.

Tired.....as usual.

- Jed

July 17th   An infiltrator is killed.......

It was bound to happen. Someone entered the neighborhood and one of the patrols shot and killed the man. The patrol, Reggie I think, was walking around the side of a house a little too close when the guy jumped him. Another patrol saw the incident approx 40 yards away and ran to assist. The guy had grabbed Reggie's rifle and they were fighting over it when Reggie let the rifle go and drew his Glock 17 before his rifle could be turned on him. Reggie's risky move paid off as he put 3 rounds of 9mm into the trespassers chest.

Reggie broke down after the shooting. He never wanted to kill someone. He kept saying that he wondered if the trespasser was someone's father, or son, or husband. He has been taken off patrol of course.

The trespassers body was taken well away from the community and buried. One of my neighbors was training to be a minister at a local Baptist church and said a few words.

Folks are beginning to understand the need for security and to take the daily tasks of neighborhood upkeep serious. This is our lives and we can't mess around.

M has lost some weight, like the rest of us. Her jeans are fitting loose around the waist so she tied them up with some paracord. Her brown hair has grown a little bit reaching just past her neckline – just like when we were back in school. Blue eyes and olive completion – simply beautiful. I am so glad she is with me.

- Jed

July 18th   Tree houses aren't just for kids.......

With the shooting yesterday folks are on edge. Depression has set in for many in the community. Life has changed so much and these people just never....and I mean NEVER thought that anything like this would ever happen. Concerns and frustrations were often limited to which outfit to wear and where to go out to eat this weekend.

Not any more.

Jessie is doing well with the kids. Activities and education are keeping them occupied. I continue to charge these small DVD players every so often and a couple times a week the kids have "Movie Night". They even pop some pop corn once in a while.

The Security Team met this afternoon and we discussed methods to get a better view around the neighborhood. We have wood from the incomplete housing sites. It was decided to build a few elevated towers throughout the neighborhood. By getting some eyes up in the air it will be easier to monitor what is going on not just in the neighborhood – but around it.

I backed the idea but warned that those in the towers would be working a very high risk assignment, which Ryan agreed. They likely could come under sniper fire from a good distance. Part of the fabrication details was to try to provide some resistance to high power rifles in the main section of the tower. I suggested that there may be a way to add some additional viewing via tree houses. I told them that with the right tree a platform could be built in the middle of the tree and the post could be camouflaged. They agreed and planned to build half as towers and half in trees.

It's a start.

I caught M crying today. I asked her what was wrong and she said she just was upset about the changes in her life. She is living in a strange place – no friends, no family. She planned her trip to the reunion and everything has been turned upside down. I tried to comfort her and told her that I was there for her. I told her - and maybe this was harsh – but the fact was that it is what it is. I told her that I am sure she will make friends here but with the world the way it is survival was the #1 priority. She looked at me like I said something wrong and said she thought I would be more compassionate. I asked her if she wanted me to lie and she said no. I hugged her and told her she had me for as long as she wanted. She said she didn't want me to get the wrong idea and that she was very glad to be with me.

I don't think I did a very good job.

- Jed

Community Talk

— Reality of the Situation
— Supplies — Food, Medicine, Water, etc.
— Gardens & Rain Capture
— Sanitation
— Defense / Security
— Working Together

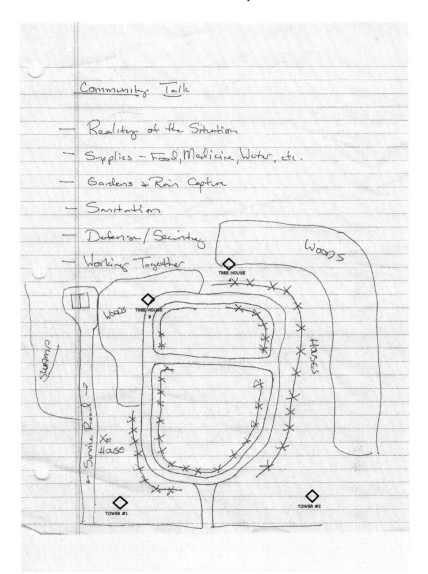

July 19th   Trouble on the home front.......

Had a large thunderstorm today with high winds. Unfortunately some of the squash plants in the garden had stalks that broke. Hopefully they are not too bad. Good thing is the rain barrels refilled. Many in the community actually went outside during the storm and stripped down to their underwear and washed up.

Eric made a water entrenchment out of some wood and plastic sheeting. Basically he built a square box 4′ x 4′ x 12″ and lined the inside with two layers of plastic sheeting. He dug the bottom down about 6 inches for more water. When it is raining he is allowing this to fill up via the rainfall. Often in hard rains the rain barrels overfill so during the next rain he will drain some from the barrels and pour the excess into the "pool". I congratulated him on a good idea. He also made a cover out of thick black plastic and some wood to keep the ultraviolet light from hitting the water. This should minimize the algae growth. Can't knock more water!

M mentioned to me that she had been talking to Jessie and Jillian (Ryan's wife). I told her that was great – hoping she was making friends. She said I might not be so glad. She said that many of the women in the neighborhood are questioning why there are only men on the Security Team and involved in patrols. I answered that I guessed that it is likely that more men have experience with firearms than women. I also told her that the patrols were put together with volunteers initially and no women signed up. She said that many women now want to contribute more and that many want to work patrols. I asked her if she was one of the ones. She said that it made her nervous but the answer was "yes". My heart sank. I stood there silent for what seemed like forever. She asked me what I thought and I was honest and said I didn't like the idea. I told her that she had little experience with firearms. She said she could be trained.

Damn, she's right.

I told her that for 20 years I dreamed of a day we would be back together again and I couldn't bear the thought of loosing her to some slime ball while out on patrol. She pointed out that I walk patrol so what is the difference?

I told her I needed to think about this and we could talk more tomorrow.

I am not sure what to do about M.

- Jed

July 20th   Rescue mission.......

Worst day in my life......

Bill and Carrie came to the house this morning at 8:00am. Hearing the knock at the door I knew something was wrong. I invited Bill and Carrie in and they told me their oldest daughter was gone. They went on to tell me that Amber, 16 years old, had left in the middle of the night to see her boyfriend. They said that she had been begging them to drive across town to see if Aaron was OK. Obviously they never took Amber. I asked how they knew that is where she went and they told me Amber left a note.

I asked if they knew where he lived and they had an address. I thought for a moment and I told them it was time to go.

I woke M and Eric up and told them what was going on and that I would be back later.

I wanted at least 3 -4 people to go. I did not want Bill to go but he was the only one who could identify Aaron. So, it was Bill, Lewis (member of the Security Team), Mark (Jessie's husband) and I. We drove the Jeep. We were all armed. Bill had a Mini-14, I had my Stag AR, Lewis brought a Winchester 70 .270 with a nice scope on it, and Mark carried my

49

Remington 870. I had a tactical vest with extra magazines. I loaned Bill a surplus AR magazine pouch. I hoped we would not run into any problems.

I punched the address in my GPS and made absolutely certain I made my way around what used to be "the bad section of town". I drove through expensive, nice neighborhoods. The destruction was awful and I began to think I had made a mistake. Large houses costing hundreds of thousands of dollars burnt up and vandalized. Windows broke, doors left wide open. Every so often a body could be seen lying in a yard or on the street. Then I came across one of the most horrible sights I have ever seen. A man was hanging from a large tree. That image was burned in my mind. Bill began to cry thinking of what may have happened to his daughter.

The GPS said 4 miles to go when we came across a car blocking the road. I didn't like the looks of this. We were approx 300 yards from the car when I stopped and pulled out my binoculars. This just didn't look right but I could not see anyone and the ways to get to where we were going was few. I inched the Jeep forward and told everyone to keep their eyes peeled in front, on both sides and behind us. When we were 50 yards from the car I switched the Jeep into 4 wheel drive planning to go around the car into peoples yards. 25 yards away I saw movement near one of the houses on the right and I floored it. The Jeep's engine jerked everyone against their seats as we lurched forward. I aimed the front of the Jeep to the left side of the car in the road – figuring the bad guys were on the right(assuming most everyone is right handed). Right when I drove up on the lawn to the left of the broken down car 3 people ran out from a house on the right side. I kept going and they started shooting. We were 10 yards past the vehicle when I heard rounds passing by and impacting the Jeep.

Bill shot out the window towards the 3 people and they dove for cover. 50 yards further away I felt something hit the back of my head. It was a strange feeling. I continued to drive and I turned to see Lewis yelling at me. I wasn't hearing him – my adrenaline and focus had been on my driving and the shots fired had my ears ringing. It was then I realized that there was something all over my neck, my right shoulder, and a little on my dashboard.

It was Mark. He was dead. One of the bullets hit Mark in the neck. He bled out quickly. He was dead.

I screamed like I never screamed before.

I looked at the GPS – 3.2 miles to go and I considered turning around to seek revenge. I considered heading home. No – we needed to try to find Amber. I drove forward. No one said anything until we were about a quarter mile away. I told Bill he needed to prepare himself for the reality that she might not be there. We turned the corner and headed down the street Aaron lived on. I estimated the house was just up on the left.

We pulled up and the house had been obviously vandalized. Windows were broke. We decided it would be best if all of us went in. I carried my Stag AR and gave Lewis my S&W M&P 9mm. I reminded everyone to keep barrels pointing in a safe direction and not to cover anyone with their gun while going through the house.

We entered the front door. I entered taking point and hit the momentary switch on my weapons mounted light. Saw nothing except broken furniture, lamps, holes in the walls, etc. We went room to room searching. I saw what looked to be blood staining the carpet downstairs. Next, we headed upstairs. I did not like this and wished I had a flash bang grenade or something. Walking up those stairs I felt like I was doing the stupidest thing I had ever done. We inched our way up and found nothing. The house was empty.

I told Bill I was sorry. He teared up. I told him lets just take a look around back. We headed out the back door. Aaron's family had a garden out back. Not much in it but there was some. We walked to the shed and opened the door. There were the typical garden tools, lawnmower, and chairs. It was right then we heard a voice – a girl's voice. She was calling out......"Daddy!!" Bill jumped back and looked to his right and ran over in that direction. I saw him suddenly look up. The neighbor had a tree house. Aaron and Amber were up in the tree house.

I need to get to sleep but to sum it up Aaron's parents were killed a few days after The Event. Aaron had been living in the tree house ever since – scavenging for food and supplies each evening. Aaron buried both his parents behind the shed. That's not all – Aaron's little brother Caleb was with him. They all came down out of the tree house and Amber ran over and hugged her father. I yelled over that we needed to go and go now. Aaron grabbed a backpack and we all headed to the Jeep. I grabbed a blanket as we went through the house and Bill and I wrapped Mark up in it. Amber screamed when she saw him. Managing to fit everyone in my Jeep we headed home.

The trip home was much less eventful. I asked Lewis if he got a good look at the 3 people that were shooting at us. He said all he could tell was that they had blue bandannas on their heads – all of them.

I am so tired. The worst of it all was having to go knock on Jessie's door – and when she opened it she knew. M took little Addie up to her bedroom and I told Jessie that Mark was gone. It didn't go well.

She blames me for his death. She's right. I shouldn't have taken anyone with kids. He was never in the military. No training at all. It was stupid. I will never forgive myself.

- Jed

July 21st Planes in the sky.......

Mark is weighing heavily on my mind. We were friends and due to my decision making he is dead. His wife is without a husband and his little girl without a father. I can't believe this has happened. I have got to just keep going. People are depending on me. I can't let up on helping get this neighborhood ready for what awaits us. M is trying to be supportive but I just want to be left alone.

I discussed M's question about women patrolling with Ryan. He felt similar to me. I guess we are old fashioned. Bill got in on the conversation and we agreed that we needed the help and there was safety – and power – in numbers. I talked to M and told her that if she really wanted to get involved she could begin training tomorrow. I told her we would start with more shooting practice and then Ryan would assist with some additional training. She wasn't really happy – more apprehensive than anything. She was so sure of herself and now that she got what she wanted she's scared. Women.....

M asked about making soap and candles. I told her I was sure I had books and we could check it out tomorrow in daylight. I have probably another 25 bars of soap, 12 bottles of liquid soap, lots of shampoo and many, many candles. I think she is trying to find a hobby. Fine by me.

I'd like to make a hobby of gorging myself with banana splits right about now!!

For the first time since The Event (3 weeks) I saw planes. Looked like a combination of jet fighters and what may have been some kind of transport – maybe a C130. They were heading West. Discussion in the neighborhood was whether or not they were ours....or someone else's. Where were they going? Who were they? What do they know? Questions asked and no answers.

Something else to think about while I am trying to get to sleep.

- Jed

July 22nd   Scouting for supplies.....and news

Amber is not taking Mark's death well. Bill told me that she is a wreck and is staying in her room. She blames herself for Mark's death and said she does not ever want to look at Jessie again. I understand. Her leaving in the middle of the night to find Aaron was a stupid thing to do. I know how she feels as well – I am finding it difficult to walk by Mark and Jessie's house – thinking of that pour little girl in there without a father.

I should have been smarter about the whole thing. Mark was a good friend and this is tearing me apart. I still can't believe he is gone.

Many people are getting low on supplies and I don't want to give away too much. I also do not want everyone to know what I have either. I talked to Ryan about going out and doing some scouting for supplies. Going and getting Amber got me thinking there are likely a lot of houses and businesses out there with supplies in them. No – not a lot of food but other things that the community needs. As I was talking to Ryan Neil walked by on the sidewalk and I saw an opportunity. I called Neil over. He stared at me like I had just eaten the last piece of cake or something. I told him we needed some help making a decision and I wanted his opinion. He looked at me like I had an angle or something and asked me to go on. I filled him in on the idea of scouting for supplies – the risk, the danger, and gave him some idea's of where we could go.

He actually spoke and said he thought it was a good idea. Neil said he had been thinking the very same thing and figured there were many businesses that may have supplies that the gangs and other low-life's may not think about. He went on to say many manufacturing facilities have vending machines, walkie-talkies, tools, welding equipment, batteries, construction stuff – even coffee. I told him that was some great thinking.

Neil smiled and his face fell off. OK, just kidding. His face didn't actually fall off. I asked him if he wanted to go if we put together a scouting party and he said he absolutely did. He went on that he was sick and tired of sitting around and working in his garden. Turned out he grew up on a farm and had a bunch of raised bed gardens in his back yard – which was fenced in like mine. He also served in the Army – was in Vietnam. I told him I was glad to have him on the "team".

The plan is to head out tomorrow to a couple local places and see what we can find. I hope it goes better than the last time we went out.

Bill came over and said that he got some news on the scanner. Basically, forces overseas are feeling the crunch to get things done due to fuel shortage problems. He said there was also talk of some of the forces breaking off and heading home. "Why?" is the question. Possibly to check on their family?

He said getting stations was difficult and most came in better after dark.

I hope tomorrow brings some positive news for a change.

- Jed

July 23rd Shocking news from the South.......

Bill came over early this morning after the sun came up. He heard news last night on the scanner and had to get it out. Mexico was left untouched by The Event – for the most part. Between the drug cartels loosing business due to the lack of money flowing in from the United States and the overall drop in the Mexican economy for the same reason – Texas and New Mexico have been invaded. By whom? Not entirely sure. Appears to be a combination of Mexican military and drug cartels.

Bill said that US citizens – especially in Texas – are putting up a heck of a fight. Violence is horrible and causalities are high – on both sides. There are minimal US military forces available and from what Bill said a small segment that are currently overseas dealing with that conflict are heading to assist in Texas and New Mexico. We both mentioned the planes we saw and figured that they may have been heading to the area.

It's been a little over 3 weeks since The Event – so much has changed. I wish I could go back in time. Preparedness would have been a much larger priority. So many things I would have stocked up on – here are a few:

- Night Vision – super expensive but would be so useful now.
- Kerosene – I have a kerosene heater and about 15 gallons of fuel. We are going to need more this winter.
- Batteries – I have a lot but could have used more. Luckily I have rechargeable ones I can charge with my small solar panel.
- Food – never enough food.
- Water Filters – I would have stocked up on more filter cartridges to build more gravity drip filter units.
- Toilet Paper – can never have enough TP.

The scouting trip was delayed until tomorrow. Everyone involved wanted to discuss exactly what kinds of things were needed, make a list, and go to those places most likely to find the stuff. Good to have a plan.

Actually had an LED flashlight stop working today. Never had that happen before. Looks like some kind of short in the lamp. Glad I have lots more.

- *Jed*

July 24th   Looting, stealing, or survival?

Bill, Neil, Eric and I went out today looking for supplies.

We have a list of items we are looking for:

- o   any tools that can be used for gardening
- o   any kind of communication tools – walkie-talkies, CB's, etc.
- o   seeds for gardens
- o   toilet paper
- o   food and water (of course)
- o   hunting/utility knives
- o   trash bags
- o   sanitation supplies - soap, body wash, shampoo
- o   first aid/medical stuff
- o   rope, string
- o   fishing supplies
- o   gardening soil/fertilizer/Round Up

We decided to go to 3 different businesses depending upon time and how the area's looked.

First – we went to a local golf course approx 3-4 miles from us called Pine Tuck. *Why?* We figured they must have some fertilizer there and if no one else had thought of it they likely would have a lot of it.

It took us about 10 minutes to get over there. We did see a few people tending to their homes and gardens. Interesting. You might have thought it was a day like any other day except there were people walking around with guns near the homes – like guards. When we arrived to Pine Tuck the clubhouse had been ransacked. No food or water. We managed to find the greens keepers shed and like we thought – found a bunch of fertilizer. Stuff was in powder form and must be applied as a liquid when mixed with water. High in nitrogen. We found some rakes and shovels as well as some riding lawnmowers. Surprisingly we were able to siphon gas out of all the mowers – no gas found anywhere else.

Next we headed 6 miles away to a local plastics manufacturer. They made some kind of packaging product. Not very many actual manufacturers around to choose from. We hit the jackpot there. Though it was obvious the place had been picked through before. I guess people were looking for something different. We found
the Maintenance Managers office and pried a filing cabinet open that was locked and found a bunch of batteries, a few sets of industrial walkie-talkies, duct tape, flashlights, rope, some chain, a few tools, and some work gloves. We also managed to find a few wall-mounted first aid kits. Good stuff.

Lastly – we headed to a small country store just outside of town called "Wilson's". Much to our surprise when we approached there were people walking around out front - and on the roof. The folks on the roof were armed and looked to be keeping order and security for the store. We all discussed what we would do and decided to approach and check it out. We pulled up and Neil and I went in while Bill sat behind the wheel of the Jeep and M in the back seat. The owners – Jake and Nancy Wilson, still had their business going and were selling and trading based on a barter system. Wilson's had a bunch of stuff - but nothing that we really needed, at least not right now. We said a friendly hello and wished them a good day.

Overall it was a good trip and we are likely to make more trips in the future. I was glad that Neil was becoming more a part of the team. He's not so bad.

One thing that someone asked – *Are we now looters?* Are we stealing from these places?

My response and opinion is we are surviving.

- *Jed*

July 25th   The world crumbles....and I am happy?

M is no longer staying in the spare bedroom. Maybe I shouldn't be writing something like that in this journal – but I am flat out happy. The world has literally crumbled around us, life has become immensely difficult – yet as I sit here under the stars trying to stay cool and lighting this journal with an LED headlamp – I am happy.

Spent part of the day with M shooting. We shot a couple of Ruger 10/22's, a Smith & Wesson 22A, and worked our way up to my Stag M4. She liked them but found her favorite was a Smith & Wesson M&P15-22 .22LR. Being so similar to an AR-15 it is a great training tool. Glad I have lots of .22LR ammo.

I am so relieved that I had stocked up on the ammunition I did. Most of the patrols in the neighborhood only have a few hundred rounds of ammo for their guns – regardless of the type. I am sitting on cases of ammo for all my guns. I don't know the exact count but thousands of rounds. I also have ammo and other supplies in the caches I have buried. I need to show M and Eric where they are located.

Need to go get some sleep.

-   *Jed*

July 26th   went "deer" hunting.......

Bill asked me if I wanted to go hunting today. Of course I went. I was never much of a hunter in my younger days. We figured much of the deer population – like the squirrels – was thinned out. He knew a place approx. 18 miles away. He said the area was not very populated so there shouldn't be very many people around.

We headed out at 9:00am – one of the latest deer hunts I have ever been on. No orange vests – and no license. I took my Winchester 94 .30-.30 lever action and he brought an old beat up .300 Savage rifle – not even sure the make. Anyways, the drive was no problem and he was right about not very many people. We headed off into the woods and walked I guess 500 yards and found a tree stand. It was one of those that you lean up against a tree and chain it off. Bill took the stand and I walked another 150 or so yards and sat down and put my back up against a tree. I was basically perched over the top of a small gully.

We stayed put for about 3 hours when it came out of the woods. I say "it" but there were more than one. I took careful aim at almost 50 yards with my open sights, controlled my breathing – and at the bottom of a breath I squeezed the trigger. That turkey had no idea what hit him as he toppled over, fluttered a bit, and laid to rest. The second one took off across the hillside towards Bill. I thought my luck couldn't get better because it was still a wide open shot. I aimed just a few inches in front of him and squeezed off another round. At the very same time I heard another shot. It was Bill. All I saw were feathers fly up in the air.

I ran down and picked up the first one shot and made my way over the second. Bill told me good shot as I walked up. I told him that I had never shot a turkey before – let alone two!! Bill asked me what I meant, because he shot the second one. Well – either way we had two turkeys.

Well, I told him either way – our families would be having a very early Thanksgiving.

I think M was very impressed with my hunting prowess when I told her the story of my shooting TWO turkeys......

 - Jed

July 27th   Blue bandanna gang pays us a visit.....

Today the patrol's alerted everyone when they saw a group of 6 men walking through the woods on the west side of the neighborhood. Glad we put those platforms in the tree's as they saw them first and alerted the patrols and other towers. It appears they were pretty much just checking us out. Once they realized they were seen – they pulled back into the woods and disappeared. I didn't see them but their one identifying trait was they all wore blue bandanas – either on their head or on one of their arms.

The FRS/GMRS radios carried by the Security Team and a few select others have really come in handy. Someone on one side of the neighborhood can talk to someone all the way on the other side. No more cell phones and these radios have been a huge help. Batteries are hard to come by but I had stocked up. Many of the radios have rechargeable in them that I charge with my small solar system.

Anyways, sounds like these folks are the same – or from the same gang - that killed Mark. I am burning up with anger and I want revenge. I know I shouldn't think like that – I have to keep control. I know myself well enough to know that I do not make the best decisions when I am angry. In times like these – wrong decisions can get someone killed.

Just ask my friend.....Mark.

Will talk with Ryan tomorrow about the visitors today. No doubt they were testing the perimeter and will continue to do so. I suspect they will be back around.

- Jed

July 28th   M has a crazy idea.....

M told me an idea today that I thought was crazy.

She asked about Aaron and Caleb moving in with us. I was shocked. Here we are just getting back together and she wants to bring kids into the house. Liable to get pretty crowded around here. She said she had been taking to Carrie, and Bill apparently is not too happy having Aaron and Amber under the same roof. After all – they are teenagers with racing hormones. M said we have an extra bedroom and Caleb and Aaron could share it. She also said we are likely the best prepared to take on a couple people – due to our food storage.

I told her I would think about it. I need to talk to Bill as well.

The heat is really doing a number on the gardens. With many gardens being planted so late seedlings are not doing well with the intense southern heat. This isn't helping with morale. The fertilizer from the golf course is being used sparingly. The best gardens are the raised beds for the most part. Soil is rich, loose, and the roots can easily crawl out in search of nutrients and moisture.

I charged up my laptop today. I am going to watch a few episodes of Seinfeld. I need a laugh.

 - Jed

July 29th   Neighbors gone.....

M and I walked the community today and knocked on doors. 20 homes in addition to the 12 that were empty prior to The Event are now vacant. Over the past couple weeks a couple of families have packed up their vehicles and headed for relatives. Biggest reason was they were running out of food.

32 homes vacant. I think that the time has come that these homes are searched for food and other supplies. Many households are getting desperate - even with rationing. Most households just never prepared for anything like this. I will talk to Ryan and Bill – as well as a few others about how to go about searching the empty houses. I think supplies found should be equally distributed to others with a request that those worse off get a little more.

One of those empty homes belongs to my neighbors – Thomas and Charlene. They took off within a couple days as Thomas had relatives down in Chester in the country. He used to talk to me about growing up on a farm and hunting year round for animals. Most of what he hunted wasn't anything I would call food. Gotta pass on the possum. He did give me my first try of wild pig. It was awesome.

M suggested that someone should write down what is taken from each house in case anyone comes back home.

I suspect dividing everything up will not be easy. The neighborhood has come together so well I would hate for fights to break out over who deserves more than someone else. It may be unavoidable.

- Jed

July 30th   The neighborhood is better off than we thought.....

I have been avoiding talking to M about Caleb and Aaron moving in. I am very uneasy about it. What would it mean to M and me? Would we become their parents? How will it affect our ability to survive? How long will our food last filling two more mouths? What about our privacy? It would be a lot of responsibility. *How about Bill?* He was already a family of four before Caleb and Aaron arrived.

M is only going to wait so long.

Started going through the vacant houses today. We talked to the neighbors to make sure that there was not anyone in the houses before we entered. Food was the main objective and a surprising amount was found. Many people left and carried only what they needed or could carry to get them where they were going, I guess. I directed the searches through each house as many things that had value to me were being overlooked by others. Beyond food – prescription meds, first aid stuff of any kinds, batteries, flashlights, fuel, tools, and even diapers were found.

12 houses out of the 32 were searched. We found a lot more food than I thought we would. Looks like some folks were out of town when The Event happened and they left a fully stocked pantry and kitchen. Lots of canned and dry goods that will keep. Numerous tools as well as a bunch of screws and nails. Hunting clothes and camping supplies were good finds as well. We even found several firearms and some ammunition.

More to check out tomorrow.

- Jed

July 31st Collecting resources....

A group of us finished going through all 32 empty houses. The ones empty prior to The Event had nothing of value. The others provided a lot more than expected.

Like yesterday quite a bit was found. More food, some very valuable antibiotics, more batteries, radios, flashlights. In particular – we found several bags of charcoal, 14 bottles of propane, and almost 30 gallons of gas in gas cans. Also found a few inverters ranging from 350 to 750 watts. I also discovered that Thomas next door still had his 4 wheeler in his shed. I brought it over and stored it in the backyard. We also came across 3 garden tillers.

Going through one of the first homes I came across a car battery sitting in the garage and I realized that there were dozens of batteries all around us that were not being used. Bill and I discussed the need to get the batteries from vacant cars and somehow use them to benefit the neighborhood. We talked to all the other Team Leaders and everyone agreed that tomorrow we would get the car batteries that were available and then work towards a method to charge them. We figured we would end up having extra's on hand which would be a good thing.

Eric worked on educating people on composting. With an inability to purchase composted cow manure and fertilizer for gardens composting will be important.

M goes on patrol for the first time tomorrow and I don't like it. She will be working a 4 hour rotation. With having more people involved in the patrols Ryan shortened the time for each patrol to 4 hours. He felt that would keep people on their feet and reduce the chance of them becoming complacent. He is also staggering the rotations so if someone is watching us they will not be able to predict the *"changing of the guard"* so to speak.

In the past several weeks so much revolves around "that which you have" and "that which you have not". It is a frustrating feeling knowing that if you had just put "X" back it would make life easier now.

- Jed

August 1st   A day of piece and quiet.....

I woke up this morning and wasn't feeling well. I think working in this heat has finally gotten to me.

I did something I probably shouldn't have – I used up a decent amount of juice from my deep cycle batteries from my solar system. I hooked up my small refrigerator, made up some Country Time Lemonade, stuck it in the fridge – and after it got cold sat back and enjoyed that cool, refreshing drink. Man....it was great.

M was patrolling our side of the neighborhood with Ryan this afternoon. When they made it to my fence I gave them each a glass. You would have thought it was Christmas. They were so surprised to feel the cold glass when I handed it to them.

Anyways – I sat around and really did little of anything. Pretty much relaxed my aching body and tried to stay cool. Read a few issues of Mother's Earth & News and SWAT magazine.

I did a lot of thinking about M, Aaron and Caleb. I guess we'll give it a shot. M has been spending a lot of time over at Bill and Carrie's. Guess she is trying to get closer to the boys.

I will tell M tomorrow and then we can talk to Aaron and Caleb. Who knows, maybe they won't want to come and stay with us.

- Jed

August 2nd   We have electricity....sorta

Turns out Neil is a hobby-electrician and was able to hook us up with a method to charge the batteries. He basically came up with the idea of using a lawnmower or edge trimmer motor along with an older alternator to charge the batteries. He said one battery can be charged at a time or the batteries can all be hooked together in series to form a battery bank. We have quite a bit of gas from vehicles left behind so we could fuel these devices for quite some time.

Neil started working on building three of these to put in different places throughout the community. Folks will be able to bring some of their own batteries plus we are providing some of the ones that we found to people. They will be able to power some lighting and other tools needed IF they have an inverter. We can also use the systems to charge batteries for the Security Team and some of the electric tools from the Gardening Team. They have some small electric tillers that work well for some of the smaller raised beds.

I think being able to flip a switch and have lighting at night will be a big morale booster. I suggested to everyone to use Christmas lights if they have them. Low power drain.

Well, I talked to M and told her I was fine with Aaron and Caleb moving in. I tried to make her aware of the responsibilities and risks with the dangers that exist today. She was not swayed at all. Neither one of us are getting any younger. We are both 39 and neither have had kids. I suspect M's motherly instincts are kicking in.

We are going to talk to Bill and Carrie tomorrow and let them know.

I'm sure Bill will be happy.

- Jed

August 3rd   The kids move in.....

M and I went over and talked to Bill and Carrie about the kids moving in with us. We had already discussed it briefly before but wanted to make sure everyone was under the same understanding. Bill and Carrie were in favor of it. M and I were in favor of it. Aaron and Caleb – not so much. Aaron wanted to stay close to Amber. I was a teenage boy once – can understand that. Caleb.....that is a tough one. He lost his parents just a few weeks ago and his life has been turned upside down. Now he is moving again.

M and I spent several hours this morning setting up a bedroom for the two of them. I remembered seeing some "cool" posters in a couple of the empty houses and brought them over to make the room a little more inviting. They came over with Bill and Carrie just after dark. Everything seemed to go pretty good.

They are in the other room – each with a small LED light. Carrie said that Caleb sometimes wakes up in the middle of the night and will yell for his Mom, and then his Dad. It is just so sad.

I am going to try to do right by these kids.

- Jed

August 4th   Ben pays us a visit.....

Ben stopped by and paid us a visit today. I had been meaning to go and visit with him and family – just hadn't had a chance. He took a look at what we were doing with the chickens he gave us a "thumbs up". We hope to have a few a few chicks running around shortly.

Ben brought us a surprise and I could not have been grateful enough. He presented me with two small hand-held HAM radios. I thanked him of course and then asked why he brought them to me. He went on to say that we are about 19 miles apart if you drew a straight line. He said that he has a pretty powerful radio with a tall antenna and he felt that we could probably talk to each other. He mentioned he bought several of these radios and could spare them. Knowing nothing about HAM radio's he showed me a few of the features on the radio and then told me to make sure I had it set for frequency 147.025 MHz. He said his radio is often on and he scans a variety of channels – and then sets it to 147.025 MHz. I suggested that we try to connect up tomorrow night at 8:00pm and see if it works.

I asked him why he brought us two and he said *you just never know*. So true. We talked for awhile; he met Aaron and Caleb and got ready to go. When he got to his truck he reached in, grabbed something, and turned around and put his hand out. I took this small silver piece of metal asking what is was. He said it's an adapter for the handheld's to mount a regular CB antenna – if I had one.

I thanked him and reminded that tomorrow night we would try to talk over the radios.

Interesting….Caleb only talked to Ben for a few minutes but he really seemed to take to him. It would be good to be able to talk to Ben once in a while. Maybe there are others I can talk to as well. Just have to figure out how to use it.

Glad to have a friend like Ben.

- Jed

August 5th   News from the scanner.....

Bill informed myself and several other community members of what he
caught on the scanner last night.

The mysterious disease affecting some folks on the West Coast has
started to spread east. Reports are coming in from Nevada and Arizona.
Same symptoms - severe fever, diarrhea, and vomiting resulting in death.
Reports state that there are scientists with the CDC trying to find a
treatment or cure.

Concerning.

Also on the scanner were reports that some state governments were
trying to remain in existence. States including Texas, Montana,
Wyoming, and North and South Dakota seem to be doing better than
others. The state governments are having minimal effects. Large cities
are struggling to maintain control over looting and mass crime. The
larger cities are the only places where curfews are actively trying to be
enforced. Just not enough law enforcement as most cops are staying at
home to be with families.

I talked to Ben tonight. At 8:00pm I turned on the BaoFeng handheld
radio to 147.025 MHz and in no time I heard Ben's voice. We talked a few
minutes. His trip home was uneventful which I was glad to hear. I told
Ben about the disease moving east. We decided to stick to talking every
Monday, Wednesday, and Friday – and monitor all other days.

After Ben and I talked I thought that we needed to use some code words
and be careful of what we say. You never know who else might be
listening. Going to look through the manual tomorrow and see what else
this radio can do.

Cool thing – Caleb came over and said he wanted to say *Hi* to Ben on the radio. One of the first times I had seen him smile.

- Jed

August 6th   We're hit, we respond.....

Almost didn't write in the journal but haven't missed a day through all of this.

We lost 4 people today. A group of 6-8 gang bangers – all wearing blue bandanna's attacked us. One small group from the North-West corner and another from the West. They came in and immediately started shooting at the towers and patrols that were in sight. Myself, Eric and several others not on patrol responded. Those in the towers were pretty much pined down. The four we lost included two patrols and an older retired couple – the Robinson's – that happened to be tending to their small garden in their backyard.

The two patrols lost were follows named Henry and Rick. I did not know them at all and I know they were both married. Not sure about kids.

The gang bangers walked right up to the neighborhood and were not seen by those in the tree houses nor the towers. A couple of things were learned from this:

- This could have been worse. As soon as the shooting started on the North-West side all the patrols covering the rest of the neighborhood ran to help. This left those area's extremely exposed.

- Friendly fire could have been an issue. All the gang members were wearing the same colors which made them easily recognizable. If not for that people may not have been able to distinguish the invaders and the "good guys".

- We have to expand our patrols to stop them from coming so close before being seen. Possibly some type of alarms.

The end result of the attack is we lost 4 people; they lost 3 and likely injured some others. I am not sure if I killed one of the gangbangers or not. One of them went down when I was shooting at them – but I was not the only one shooting.

Strange....I do not feel guilty. The Robinson's and the patrols that lost their life today made sure of that.

- Jed

August 7th   Some neighbors ask for help.....

We had a visitor at the front entrance today that asked for me by name. His name - Karl Faile. We were friendly at the YMCA when I was a member and we played some racquetball together. That was a couple of years ago and he gave me a ride home once when my car wouldn't start.

One of the patrols radioed me on my FRS/GMRS radio. I rode my bike up to the entrance way and barely recognized Karl. He was much thinner than I remember. The patrols checked him for weapons and we walked up to the house. Over some lemonade-flavored water he brought me up to date on his situation.

Karl, his wife Samantha, and two boys Christopher and Jonathan live about 2 miles away. He said they have not had any problems and very few visitors. He said the street they live on has 18 homes and is right off a long stretch of road with no houses or businesses. He said most of the families have lived there for quite a while and knew each other. All are church-goers and have been helping each other out any way they can. Luckily – they also have several wells – so water has not been an issue. Food is the main problem. They are all rationing severely and although many of the folks there had gardens – crops had gone by. Karl looked at me and asked if there was anything we could do to help.

I told him that I did not speak for the entire neighborhood – and would have to talk with others before answering. I was honest with him and emphasized that we may be doing better than them but was not sure how much we could do to help.

I decided to drive Karl home. We got in the Jeep and headed out. He was right about his street. I had never driven down it before but had seen it. The drive down the long road he described was approximately 1 mile, then his street – Walnut Street – was just on the left. I could see if people had started walking down the long road they likely would turn around seeing no houses or anything.

Walnut Street had 18 homes – 8 on each side and then 2 on the end. These were country homes – most single story. Yards were overgrown with grass but beyond that you would never know The Event ever took place. Along the way I filled Karl in on some of the news coming in on the scanner. He asked me a million questions and was so excited for news. They had not heard anything in several weeks and their FM radios broadcasted nothing but static.

I told him it may be a couple of days but I would get back with him.

I drove away thinking about Karl, Samantha, and their two boys Christopher and Jonathan. I want to do something to help – but we cannot risk ourselves in the process.

I gave Karl a few MRE's as he got out of the Jeep. He actually got choked up.

This is going to be tough.

- Jed

August 8th   A bartering system comes together.....

I called a neighborhood meeting this morning. Everyone met at 2:00pm at the model house. I filled everyone in on Karl's street including the situation they are in and that they are asking for help – of any kind.

Although I led the meeting which accounted for close to 75% of the residents – I emphasized that whatever decisions made we must not sacrifice the survivability of the community. A few of us mentioned that no doubt Walnut Street needed food more than anything, but they actually had something we could use.....water.

We continue to filter water from the "swamp" near the utility road, but the water has to be boiled and our filter materials are running low. Their well-water could really help us out.

People were supportive of providing assistance but rightly showed concern about donating food that we really couldn't afford to give away. Ryan suggested that we could go on a couple more scouting trips looking for supplies from abandoned homes, businesses, etc. to trade off to Walnut Street and help them out. The decision was made to go on a scouting trip tomorrow to look for supplies and then make a decision as to help Walnut Street or not.

It's a tough situation. Many of us want to help Karl's people out but we have to look out for ourselves first. With that in mind I am going to suggest something a little different before we leave.

- Jed

August 9th   Scouting trip.....

This morning I met with Ryan and explained to him my thinking on helping Walnut Street. I told him that I know I was the one that brought all this forward but it sounded to me like the scouting idea was "us" taking on all the risk and them reaping all the rewards. I suggested that Bill and I go over to see Karl and tell them about the scouting idea. If they are in favor then they needed to share the workload and risk.

Ryan agreed.

Bill and I drove over and saw Karl. We filled him in on the idea to scout for supplies and assist them in getting organized and going in the right direction. We are certainly not living in paradise but better than most. We told Karl we could all work together so it is mutually beneficial. We told him we wanted water from the wells.

Karl thanked us and said he appreciated our willingness to help. He walked across the street to his neighbor Brian's house. They both walked back shortly thereafter. We made introductions, discussed the details of our scouting trip, and headed out.

I didn't like bringing Karl due to him having kids. Since I didn't know anyone else I really didn't have a choice. On this trip only Bill and I were armed.

The first place we stopped at was a small country/restaurant store just East on Hwy 901. Of course the place had been ransacked but we took a look anyways. It is amazing what people will walk by and not see. We found several large bags of rice and beans. We also found salt, couple small bags of sugar and some flour. I guess the folks that went through the place before looked at a bag of dried beans and had no clue what to do with it. Also picked up a couple bottles of cooking oil. Lastly – they had a bunch of empty food grade buckets that looked like pickles and other things were stored in.

Second place was a small welding/mechanics shop. Not much of value found here other than a portable welder that could come in handy. No food or drinks. Vending machine had been smashed in and everything taken.

The last place we went to was a manufacturing facility on Cel-River Road that had closed down recently. The place had graffiti painted all over the sides of the building. We managed to bust a window and make our way in. Similar to the plastics plant we searched a few weeks ago we found a lot of items of value. More walkie-talkies, batteries, gloves, and some wall mounted first aid cabinets. In the office area there was a fridge which still contained some water, a few soda's, and canned fruit. We also came across some 12 volt car batteries. The maintenance shop had a lot of wire which was needed. Walking through the offices I found something which I saved to give to M. I hope she likes it.

We made our way back to Karl's place and split everything pretty even except for the rice and beans which we gave 75% to Walnut Street. Several folks came out of their homes and were very thankful. I told Karl I would be back tomorrow to get some water and talk.

I think these scouting trips need to be more frequent. Problem is the risk of traveling and eventually we are liable to enter a building that is already occupied.

- *Jed*

August 10th   Trip to Walnut Street and M's surprise.....

I borrowed a trailer from one of the neighbors and pulled it over to Karl's place. I had a couple empty 55 gallon drums that held some kind of floor wax at one time as well as a boat-load of 5 gallon buckets and tops. Made a couple trips filling everything up with well water. The 55 gallon drums had been washed out previously with Simple Green and rinsed several times before the event. Likely will not use the water for drinking – at least not yet.

While at Karl's I discussed several of the things we have done in the neighborhood as well as much of the news that has been heard. Turns out that the Walnut Street people have few firearms – couple shotguns, some .22LR's, and a few pistols. Karl himself has a Ruger 10/22 with a partial box of ammo and one 10-round magazine. Discussed some ideas for security – setting up patrols and such. Also talked about communication. They have a couple walkie-talkies from the trip yesterday as well as a few FRS/GMRS handhelds. Most of the folks still had some fuel in their vehicles. Karl said they were scared to venture out much. I told him about our building battery banks and setting up charging stations. He is going to ask his neighbors to see if anyone has the skills to duplicate our efforts.

Told Karl I would be back in a couple days for some more water and if he needed help with the battery banks I would be glad to help.

This evening I gave my surprise from yesterday to M. We ate dinner – outside by candlelight like usual. Glad I stocked up on OFF bug spray. Dinner was beef stew over rice. Getting tired of it but still good. Anyways, after dinner I told M I had a surprise for her. Tried to get her to guess – kinda fun. Went inside and brought out a small box. She opened it.......
"chocolate!!!"

I had found a few Hershey bars. She hugged me and immediately scoffed one down. Amazing how she appreciated something that just a couple months ago she wouldn't have given a second thought.

Overall – good day.

- *Jed*

August 11th   The future.....

This morning I woke up thinking about the future. What does it hold? How will this small neighborhood make it? What about Karl, his family, and the rest of Walnut Street? What about Ben? What about the children of today like Aaron and Caleb? So many questions and so few answers.

Can this country rebuild? Can it rebuild to be something even better than it was before? I guess there is not much I can do about the rest of the country but maybe right around here something can be done. It has only been a little over a month since nuclear bombs detonated in 12 cities in this country. Chemical weapons were used on other targets to create mass terror and several major electrical power stations were bombed. The community beyond this neighborhood needs to try to come together.....somehow.

I decided to go see Karl again. I talked to him about going to see Ben. We drove down to Ben's place and was welcomed by those same signs on his fence – "If you can read this you are within range!" Love that. Ben was happy to see me. Over some warm sweet tea I talked to Ben about what has been going on recently, including Karl's street. I also talked to both of them about the need for the community to start coming together and the sooner the better it will be for everyone. Ben agreed and asked how we should get started.

I told him the first involved communication. We have my place, Karl's place, and Ben's place. We need to form a communications network to share news and information. I asked Ben if it was OK if I gave Karl one of the handheld HAM radio's that he gave me. Ben said that was fine by him. I figured that the three of us would be able to communicate and that could be the start of a new communications system in the area.

Next – and probably the most important....is God. We need to create a place to worship and give thanks to God. Though services may not be held on a regular basis – it needs to be done. Karl and Ben agreed. I told them that one of my neighbors had been training to be a minister before The Event. I think his name is Joel.

We finished the meeting with a prayer, shook hands and agreed to meet up again in a week. This endeavor needed some brainstorming.

I dropped Karl off at his place and headed home. Before leaving I gave him a 100-rd. box of CCI Mini-Mag's for his Ruger 10/22 and a BX-25 25-rd. magazine. He was very thankful. When I got home M met me at the door, worried because I was gone so long. We crawled into bed and I told M my thoughts on the community – and getting started on moving forward instead of falling behind. She said she was proud of me and from what she had seen of me since the reunion....if anyone could make it happened it was me.

Wow!

- Jed

August 12th   Communication from the East.....

Reading some information I had saved before The Event I managed to connect in to a repeater today using my HAM radio. Glad the repeater is still powered up. I actually talked to someone who lives about 90 miles east of here. Said his name was David and was a member of a survival group in Pickens County. He would not provide very many details of the group which is understandable.

We talked briefly. I was able to share the conditions in the Rock Hill area and I was able to learn that his area was similar. While talking I wrote down a few things:

- First 3 weeks after The Event things got extremely violent. Hunger, sudden lifestyle change, and lack of communication caused many law abiding citizens to commit crimes ranging from assault to murder.
- David's group had to defend their property - approx 12 acres – from many that wanted to take what they have. They had prepared to an extremely high level for conditions just like this.
- Similar to my thinking – David's group is linking up with others to network and develop some kind of resemblance of community. Several small groups have linked and trade off skills and supplies and work together to provide security as well.
- He also has heard of the disease from the West.
- Gangs of brigands, hoodlums, and criminals seem to be growing in size, creating a larger threat.
- David mentioned that there was someone stating that they were a representative from the local government - calling himself the "Mayor" and trying to collect taxes and supplies. He said this "Mayor" was not elected and seemed to not be working in the best interest of the people.
- We both wonder what the total death toll is since The Event.

We wished each other well and ended our conversation.

- Jed

August 13th   Aaron and Caleb are fitting in.....

Spent quite a bit of time with Aaron and Caleb today. I talked with them about the need for "work" to keep everything around the house and the neighborhood going. Chores were something they were not really used to before The Event – and have lived through some incredibly tough times since.

Caleb is a good little kid and I feel a growing connection with him. I can't imagine what it would be like to experience what Caleb has at 9 years old. He continues to wake up at night yelling for his Mother or Father – and then fall asleep crying when he remembers the reality of what has happened in his life.

I did some basic firearms training with both the kids today. I introduced them to my Daisy 881 pellet rifle and covered and emphasized safety with them. They got sick of me telling them *"Finger off the trigger until ready to shoot."* Both did well.

After lunch M, the kids, and I got together in the shade of the garage and talked. I asked them to give me some ideas on chores that they should be responsible for. Trying to get them motivated and on-board by allowing them to make some decisions. We put together a list for each and agreed that starting tomorrow the workload would be split up.

One thing I was particularly surprised at was Aaron brought up Mrs. Williams that lives on the other side of the neighborhood. She is an older woman that lives alone. Aaron said he would volunteer to check on her each day and see if there was anything she needed done around her house. I asked him why he was so interested in Mrs. Williams. He said she was really nice and reminded him of his Grandmother whom he was very close too. She passed away a couple years ago when he was 14. I told him I thought that was a great idea and I was very proud of him for thinking of others.

He then said he wanted to go see Amber. Teenage love – I remember those times.

Tonight M and I sat holding hands watching Caleb draw. She looked at me and smiled. The smile was different. It seemed to communicate "Thank you" and "I am happy" at the same time. It is hard to explain – but it was like she was accepting that this is her home and this is her life.

- *Jed*

August 14th   Bill confesses.....

Bill and I drove over to get more water and discuss a few things with the folks on Walnut Street. While we were filling some of the containers we started talking. Something popped in my head -not sure why. I asked him what happened to all the prisoners at Moss Justice Center where he worked as a Correction Officer.

Bill looked at me very strangely and asked me what I meant. I said that since the officers slowly stopped coming to work – as well as himself – what happened to the prisoners?   He looked at me again and his chin started quivering. I walked over to him, putting my hand on his shoulder – told him that he didn't need to tell me but if he wanted to I would listen.

Bill spilled it. He described the situation as himself and a few other officers showed up the last day. They all talked about filling their vehicles from the facility pumps with gas – and heading home to stay. The violence and gang activity was getting too severe and the priority needed to be with their families. I agreed as he continued.

Bill said that they scavenged numerous supplies, filled their tanks – and discussed what to do with the 185 prisoners left inside. The decision was made to let most of them go. I asked him what he meant by most of them.

He said the few that were accused of murder, sexual crimes involving children, and rape – they never left. Tears streamed down his face. I told him it was OK and he could stop. He said he wanted to talk and that he has not told a soul since that day. He said there were six inmates identified that their crimes could not justify their being released. He said they were all killed, and he hung his head.

Bill went on to say that only three officers had shown up the last day and they each took two inmates. He said he lies awake hearing the begging from two inmates that he killed. Bill said they all had talked and with what was going on – what if they released them and they ended up raping, or killing someone else. What if they hurt a member of our family? He said they did what they felt like they had to do but they were not happy about it.

I told Bill decisions likely could not get much tougher than that and I did not look at him any different. I told him that he is a good Father and he was looking out for his own kids as well others.

He looked up at me and asked, *'What if they were innocent?"*

I had no response.

- Jed

August 15th   What if we need to bug out?

Things are going decent in the neighborhood. We have contacts a couple miles away (Walnut Street) as well as Ben down in Chester. M asked me today – *What if a large gang comes and overwhelms us?*

Good question.

We talked a bit and decided we needed to be prepared in case the need to leave in a hurry arises. In the Jeep I have some supplies – the same supplies I had when M and I left Athens after The Event. There is a BOB (bug out bag), spare fuel, water, maps, some tools, extra serpentine belt, small air compressor, and a few more things. Really need to have more supplies ready if we are to leave and not come back.

Worked on it some today and hopefully will finish by this weekend. I pulled the small flat trailer out from behind the shed in the backyard. Inflated the tires and cleaned it off and moved it in the garage. Basically I am setting up the trailer to be able to hook it up to the Jeep and head out – pronto! The trailer will hold the supplies we will take to our destination. *Where will that be?* Man, I really should have planned all this out – even before The Event happened.

Today I brought in quite a bit of deck wood that I had stored behind the shed and will use it to build up some walls on the trailer as well as provide divided areas on the trailer to store stuff. I have several totes already being used to store things. The totes can be attached to the trailer as well.

Brainstorming here – will need to consider:

- shelter
- food
- water
- medical
- defense
- clothing
- cooking
- sanitation
- information
- light
- power
- fire starting
- general supplies

Not sure how complete I can cover all those categories on one trailer and inside my Jeep. Prioritizing will be necessary.

- Jed

August 16th   Bug out trailer coming together.....

Worked hard today on the bug out trailer. Managed to use the deck wood to build up the sides as well as create sections which to store things and keep them in place/organized. Everything will be covered by tarps and tied down.

M has been helping organize some things specifically for the trailer. I asked her this morning to make a list of those things that she felt should be priority. She was kind of excited and I think proud that I asked for her opinion. She turned around and asked the boys their opinion as well – so everyone is involved.

Eric hasn't been spending as much time around the house. He usually is walking the neighborhood helping others with their gardens and keeping people informed of things. He has really grown up and matured. Taking on the leadership of the Gardening Team did wonders for him. I am not sure where Eric is spending his evening hours as he is not coming home until after dark.

Talked to Karl tonight over the HAM for a few minutes. He said things are coming together with his neighbors. Told him I will stop by sometime within the next few days.

- Jed

August 17th   Missing weather reports.....

I miss being able to click on a weather app on my cell phone and know what the weather will be for the day – or the week. A storm came rolling through – high winds, torrential downpours. I wondered for a bit if a hurricane might have hit the coast and headed inland like Hugo did way back when. Got me thinking about this winter. Although we may get flurries every year -an occasional ice or snow storm does happen. Would be great to be able to get a heads up on something like that coming.

A group went out today scouting for supplies and came back with some useful items. They found some empty 55 gallon plastic drums, extension cords, a few car batteries, blankets, jackets - minimal food and no fuel.

I went on my own scouting trip today – M not too happy about it. Aaron went with me. We drove up the road a few miles to where there are some railroad tracks. I had remembered seeing something that would be useful for the trailer. When we arrived at the tracks there was what I had remembered seeing – a solar panel. I am not sure what it was used for – possibly some kind of sensor for the tracks. We unbolted the panel and brought it back to the Jeep. I decided to drive to another intersection where there was another track – and found another panel. After that we headed back to the house.

Place is like a ghost town. As we drove around there we no other cars on the streets. We saw more burned out houses and evidence of violence. We saw a few people walking near homes – but that was it. Just so strange.

Aaron said he was glad to get out and it was good for us to spend some time together. I have been feeling a lot closer to Caleb – and maybe that is natural since he is just a little kid and Aaron is a lot older. I explained to Aaron that the solar panels would be mounted on the trailer. Several batteries would be charged by the panels and then hooked to an inverter as a power source. He thought the idea was pretty "swag". Not sure what that means but I guess it is good.

Another thing Aaron and I did was look over my preparedness library. Before The Event I had bought a lot of books. I also printed out many articles and manuals and put them in 3-ring binders and organized them by category. I also have my Kindle Fire loaded up with books and pdf's. Lastly – I have a couple of external hard drives and USB thumb drives full of stuff. With power scarce – glad I have the books and binders. Aaron asked if he could read some of them and I told him no problem.

- Jed

August 18th   Eric has a girlfriend.....

Figured out why Eric had been spending so much time away from the house....he has a girlfriend.

He told me today that he has been spending a lot of time with a women on the other side of the neighborhood. Her name is Pam. I remember seeing her before The Event but had never talked to her. Eric told me that he helped her with a couple of raised bed gardens and during the time at her place – something just clicked. I told him that was great and I was happy for him. He mentioned they are talking about moving in together but she is concerned about the limited food supplies she has.

This is tough. The neighborhood has come together and helped each other out, but I cannot basically take in another mouth to use up the supplies I have. I told Eric that if he decided to move in with Pam I would support him the best I can. He can certainly take some supplies with him. He said that he felt that his moving was likely to happen.

Interesting..... "Dating during a disaster". If electricity was still on this would make for a reality show.

Finished up quite a bit of work on the bug out trailer. M is making up an inventory list which I might slip into this journal for future reference. I watched her with Caleb earlier today. She was beautiful. I am surprised that she never had kids of her own. Seems to come natural to her.

Short entry today. Tired and need to get to sleep.

 - Jed

August 19th   Bug out trailer complete and ready.....

Talked to Ben earlier about the bug out trailer. Mentioned we planned to head somewhere near Chester State Park. He asked me why don't I just come to his place if the need arises. I told him that would be great and I really appreciated it. He mentioned that he could always use the help around the farm and numbers mean security.

Hopefully his offer won't be needed.

Went through the house and organized many items – from shelves, out of cabinets, and staged all items on the trailer. Several totes and Roughneck containers hold everything. Everything is organized by categories:

- Food – Six totes contain various canned goods; freeze dried foods, and other food items.
- Water – Ten cases of water are laid out as well as 20 2-liter bottles that are full. One of my homemade Berkey-type water filters is also included.
- Shelter – Several tarps as well as a **large tent** are stored.
- Light – One tote contains numerous flashlights, lanterns, and candles. Lot's of extra batteries as well.
- Medical – Another tote contains first aid/medical stuff.
- Fire/Cooking – A Dutch oven, pots, pans, mess kits, various cooking tools, eating utensils, and fuel are divided up between two totes. Of course – my Deadwood Stove is a must.

- Defense- A few of my extra firearms are pre-staged on the trailer along with ammunition, magazines, and some other accessories. If something were to suddenly happen to where we needed to bail I would hope I would already be armed and take my main defensive firearms with me in the Jeep.
- General – One tote contains various items such as mosquito netting, insect repellent, knife sharpening stuff, walkie-talkies, couple radios, some books and information binders, rope, paracord, binoculars, etc.
- Knives – Small tote full of various knives.
- Clothes – Larger tote contains extra clothes for everyone in the house – including extra shoes. A few sleeping bags and blankets are also thrown in a large trash bag.

The floor of the trailer is pretty much covered. I mounted the solar panels along the back positioned in the middle. Needed to do this as the entire top of the trailer is covered by a couple of tarps. Just under the panels are 3 car batteries along with a charge controller and an inverter. The batteries can be plugged into the electrical system of the Jeep so the batteries will actually be charged while driving, then the solar panels can charge them while at camp.

Overall I am pretty happy with the system. Basically we can travel to our destination and set up camp. Limited power would be available. We can purify water. We can cook food. It would be a start.

A lot more than many people have.

So – it sits in the garage and it's ready to go.

- Jed

August 20th   Thinking of Fall & Winter.....

I ran into Jessie today. M and I were walking down the street to see Eric and Pam. Jessie was coming over from another neighbor's house. I stopped and asked her how she and Addie were doing. She started to walk by and not say anything, then she turned – and said they were OK. I told her if she needed anything....anything at all – to please come over. She said OK and continued to her house.

It was a lot cooler today than it has been. Only reached in the mid-70's. Felt Fall-like and that got me thinking about the winter. With no electricity it is going to be a cold one. I have plastic sheeting stored to put on windows, a kerosene heater in the shed along 30 gallons of kerosene, two small propane heaters and quite a few small propane cylinders. Stuff just isn't going to last long if over used. Probably need to close off some of the least used rooms once it gets cold to keep heat in where we are most of the time. Luckily the winters here are usually pretty mild – though the nights can be frigid.

One of the patrols stationed in a tree house saw a couple people sitting in the woods using binoculars – watching. They appeared unarmed though they may have had pistols. The tree house radioed the ground patrols which caused a pair of patrols to respond. The people in the woods turned and left.

- Jed

August 21st   Walnut Street is attacked.....

The folks on Walnut Street went weeks with no problems – until last night. Karl radioed me this morning and I drove over. He told me a group of 4-6 men right at dark forced their way into two homes and killed the people living there. There were no initial gun shots – those poor folks were stabbed. Karl said he heard screams and went to investigate. He was met up by the two patrol's they had walking the neighborhood at that time.

They walked in the general direction of the screams and heard a ruckus inside one of the homes. With very little light out the two patrols approached from the front while Karl walked around back. One of the patrol's saw the front door broke and started blowing his whistle. Apparently that is their signal to the rest of the people on the streets. As soon as the whistle was blown a couple of the guys inside shot in the direction of the sound and then ran out back. Karl said they were fast and bolted out the back door and into the woods.

Karl – not knowing what happened to the people inside – did not fire any shots as they exited the homes. I asked him if he got a look at them. He said one thing is they were all wearing blue bandannas.

Hearing who was involved.....I was enraged. Whoever these people are they are likely wreaking havoc all over the area. They killed my good friend Mark. They killed four others in another attack a few weeks ago. Now they have killed others trying to just live. Just trying to live.

They must be dealt with. They need to be taken out before they hurt more innocent people. Who knows – they hit our neighborhood once, they may hit it again.

Tomorrow going to talk to Bill and Ryan about this. We need to find out more about this gang. Where do they live? How many of them are there? How well are they armed?

I feel this pressure in my chest. It is anger and frustration. If this community and area is to ever get some resemblance of normalcy – we can't accept these kinds of people exiting near us. Going to have a hard time getting to sleep.

- Jed

August 22nd   Successful hunting trip.....

This morning one of my neighbors – Kenny - came around and said he was heading out to do some hunting. Hunting is something that we have been doing – but mostly unsuccessful. There are not nearly as many squirrels and rabbits around as there used to be. Kenny said he knew of an area that he hunted with some friends – fairly remote.

Kenny showed me on a map where the hunting area was. Looks to be approx 14 miles south towards Chester – risky. We talked about it for a bit and decided to go. I packed up some food and water to take along and we took the Jeep. Not the best tool for the job, I decided to use my Stag Arms M4 5.56mm carbine. Reason is nowadays you just never know what...or who you will run into when in the woods. I want the firepower of the Stag.....just in case.

Bill decided to come along as well. We all had Midland FRS/GMRS radios. We arrived to the woods at 7:30am. I pulled the Jeep into the trees – about 20 yards off the road. We walked in and decided to split up to cover more area. Kenny had some scent cover and we all used it.

I took the northern direction and walked for close to 1/2 mile. I came across a ridge that overlooked a small ravine between two hills. Decided to sit atop the ridge and just watch. I hate doing nothing. I started thinking about all the things that have happened in the past several weeks. The reunion, The Event, traveling back home from Athens with M, getting the neighborhood together, Mark's death. I had always tried to prepare for something like this but as I look back on it now....I was not even close to being prepared. Now M is living with me....we are a couple again. Eric is moving in with Pam. M and I have two "adopted" kids with Aaron and Caleb. All of this in just the last several weeks.

At that point I heard a shot from the East. Must be Kenny. I watched and listened. Within a minute or so 5 deer came running over the opposite hill and down toward the valley. I could not immediately tell doe from buck. I raised the Stag M4 up and placed the red dot from my Vortex Strikefire on the first deer. I squeezed the trigger and immediately targeted another. I shot again and moved the dot to another deer. They were about to go around a bend and disappear into cover when I decided to let loose. I placed the red dot on fur and started cranking out shots.

I'm glad I brought the M4 and not my Winchester .30-30.

When I looked back to where I first started shooting I saw one small deer lying down at the bottom of the ravine. My heart jumped with excitement. I ran down to the path the deer were running and saw blood. I followed it around the bend where they ran to and there was another deer – this one a buck – laying dead. Two deer!! I could believe it.

I radioed Kenny and Bill. The first shot I heard – Kenny got a doe as well. Three deer in one day. Awesome!!

We arrived back home around 3:00pm. A couple people in the neighborhood, including Kenny, knew how to butcher the deer. Once the meat was obtained – Bill, Kenny and I decided to have a community cook out. We had all this meat and no way to refrigerate it long term. M, Aaron and Caleb walked the neighborhood and notified everyone. At 8:30pm we were grilling out. People arrived to the smell of venison cooking on a pair of propane grills (one mine, the other Bill's – I let him use one of my tanks). M and I ground up some of the wheat I had stored away and made several loaves of bread. We split all the meat up with people in the neighborhood. Much of it went into stews to spread the flavor as far as we could. Canned vegetables help complete the stew. Everyone got a some - and Bill, Kenny and I each got a piece of steak for our efforts. A few bottles of wine came out and were shared as well.

Tonight was the first time I have seen many of these people not just smile....but laugh. It was really a great time and for a few moments many of us forgot about the changes that our lives have been through.

- Jed

August 23rd   We are paid a visit.....

A man and woman came to the front entrance today asking to speak to whoever was in charge. I was radioed as well as Ryan. Jumped on my mountain bike and headed up to see what was going on. The couple's names were Phil and Lisa. Ryan and I introduced ourselves after they did the same.

They said they represented another neighborhood just south of us on Hwy 72. A small community of 30 families outside the city limits. Several of the families have chickens, goats, rabbits and a few cows. They said they were Christians and looking to reach out to others in an attempt to not just rebuild, but come together to help provide security for each other and survive. They said that they have had scouts watching us and felt from what they have seen that we were good people. We are the first neighborhood contacted.

I asked them about their defensive capabilities. Firepower is lacking as they mostly have weapons best suited for hunting – long barreled shotguns, bolt action rifles, bows, and some muzzle loaders. They are 12 miles south and off a side road of a side road. They have had a couple of run in's with trespassers but no causalities. They admitted they have been lucky and feel it is just a matter of time.

I told Phil and Lisa that I would have to talk to the rest of the neighborhood. I asked specifically what they wanted. They said that they could share some of their food as well as provide a few animals over time in exchange for security assistance. They said there may be other ways that we could mutually benefit each other as well.

I asked them when the last time they had paid us a visit. Phil said it was a couple days ago they had come through the woods and were spotted and took off.

I told Phil and Lisa that I would need a few days to talk to everyone and get back with them. They drew me a map to their location, asked if we could pray together, and left. They had a car parked off the road a couple hundred yards away.

Ryan and I talked. We both felt that they were awfully trusting – too trusting. Regardless – we are very curious.

- Jed

August 24th Neighborhood meeting, coyotes, and hunting trips planned.....

A meeting was organized for the entire neighborhood. Ryan and I discussed the offer from Phil and Lisa with everyone and made some recommendations.

The recommendations offered was for a small party to travel to the Hwy 72 community and see where they live, meet more of the people there, check out the land layout, and discuss matters more. We asked for additional suggestions and a few spoke up:

- Mike (Jennifer's husband from the other side of the neighborhood) said the deal sounds awfully suspicious to him and he was very nervous.
- Joel – who was training to be a minister prior to The Event – said that he was happy to hear that Phil and Lisa emphasized

their Christian faith. He also volunteered to make the "inspection trip".

- Neil, who always has an opinion – said that he agreed with the inspection trip but said we need to be extremely careful. He also said that it was very true that we could use their help providing sustainable food.

The decision was made to go and visit Sunday. Who exactly would go has not been decided.

- – – – – – – –

Last night I was woke up by a yelping, high pitched sound. It sounded like coyotes. In all my years here I have only seen one coyote around and it was lying dead on the side of the road a couple miles from here. This morning I walked the perimeter of the fence and saw some tracks. Looks like coyotes were right outside the fence. I couldn't tell how many.

I am guessing they are getting hungry. The rabbits and squirrel population has been reduced in the area. The cookout we had the other night probably did not help either and brought them in closer. Will pass my observations along to everyone.

- – – – – – – –

Kenny stopped by this evening and said he was planning to make another trip and asked if I would go. I suspect he is wanting me to drive as I don't think he has any gas. I told him I would very much like to go and I wanted to research out what could be done to preserve the meat rather than cooking it all.

Going to start planting some Fall crops here pretty soon. Need to look into that tomorrow.

- Jed

August 25th Military heading home.....

Bill came over and brought the shortwave radio. Big news from overseas.
All US military forces are heading back to the United States.
 Tremendous damage has been inflicted on Iran, North Korea, and China.
The countries have been blasted almost into one big parking lot and there
is little else to do. US military supplies are running low and with no
manufacturing going on of anything, anywhere......they are heading
home.

All of Europe and the Middle East are struggling. Economies have totally
collapsed with no exporting, no importing. Massive riots and violence
have led to martial law throughout. Religious wars have broken out as
many groups looked at this as an opportunity – especially in the Middle
East. They know the United States is distracted.

The world is in chaos – and our troops are coming home. They deserve it.

What will they find? What will they do? Will they arrive to their homes
and find their families waiting for them or will they find the home empty,
desolate, and lonely?

Sometimes I do not realize how lucky I am. Lying beside me M sleeps as I
write in this journal. We still have food, a shelter over our heads, solar
power, clean water, seeds, Aaron and Caleb, and each other. So much
more than most and much more than many of those brave serviceman
that have served this country.

I guess I am feeling philosophical. Each day that goes by is one day closer
to.....what? What should I expect? What can I expect? What can we hope
for? Will we ever go back to "normal"? I doubt it. Can electricity ever be
restored? Can hospitals reopen? Will the government run a 1 trillion
dollar deficit again? Who knows?

What I know for sure is we need to exist. We need to survive. We need to love and care for each other – all of us. And we need to fight evil should it make the mistake of crossing paths with us. We – as a people – need to be determined to carry on. We need to praise God for what we have and pray that he will show us the way.

That's enough for tonight.

- Jed

August 26th   Visit to Hwy 72.....

The neighborhood had its first Church service this morning. Joel organized the service at the model house. A lot of people showed up and it went well. I think if Joel keeps these services going it will do a lot to build the closeness of the neighborhood where it needs to be.

Joel, Ryan, Kenny and I drove down Hwy 72 this afternoon. We met with Phil and Lisa. Amazingly – although it was not easy to find - we just drove in the front entrance. No guards or patrols. A couple other families came walking to greet us shaking hands and hugging us. Ryan and I looked at each other and we both could tell we were getting a little creeped out. At that point Joel stepped out of the Jeep and there was a sudden, awkward pause in the greetings – just for a brief but obvious moment.

Phil led us to an old red barn where we met up with three other men. There names were John, Josh, and Rick. As we walked around I saw chickens roaming in a small pen, a few cows inside a fence-line, and a few goats. Inside the barn there were horse stalls and several horses. Phil and the other men from Hwy 72 said they were glad to meet us and hoped we could come to a mutually beneficial arrangement. They went on to explain that although they have had limited run-ins with trespassers - they are worried and concerned. During their discussions one of them made the statement – "We know there has been a lot of violence and break ins, especially by some of those ni..... err..... people."

Ryan looked at me and I spoke up. I told them I was going to lay the cards on the table and asked what was going on. A couple of them looked at Joel – who happens to be black. I demanded to know why they were looking at Joel. Phil spoke up and said to please excuse their manners – that they were not used to being around....... "their" kind. I told all of them the meeting was over and that we were not going to help or conduct business with racists. Ryan agreed, as well as Kenny – and we turned to head out of the barn.

I made myself very aware of the location of my M&P9 pistol on my hip. We walked out of the barn and got in the Jeep and left. Before we left I told Phil we had nothing else to say and to stay away from us. Phil said nothing but had a look of anger.

I was so disappointed. I really wanted this to work out as they could have benefited us so much. I wonder what the neighborhoods reaction will be as I think some hopes were high.

- Jed

August 27th Eric moves in with Pam, and rabbits.....

Eric has settled in with Pam. We moved the last of his stuff today. I told him that I was very proud of him and that I knew Dad would be proud as well. He took along a decent amount of food. I walked down to their place this evening and gave Eric a present- a Springfield XD9 – 9mm semi-automatic pistol. I also gave him a couple hundred rounds of ammo.

Other than the XD9 – Eric's only other gun is a stock Ruger 10/22. Hopefully he won't NEED to use either one.

I surprised Eric with the pistol – he surprised me with rabbits. Yes, rabbits. He managed to catch a couple and built a cage behind Pam's house. He has a male and female. He is hoping they do what rabbits do and soon will have little rabbits. He actually used a wooden box turned upside down and lifted on one end with a stick. He tied a string to the stick, baited it and spent yesterday morning and afternoon waiting. The rabbits hopped.... the string is pulled, the box falls and the rabbit is trapped.

The neighborhood was not very happy with what happened on Hwy. 72. I am tired and need to hit the sack so not going to get into a lot of details, but folks had their hopes up. Maybe I overreacted. I mean, maybe I should have been more patient and discussed the deal. Ryan felt the same way as me while Kenny said flat out we did the right thing. Joel did not say a whole lot other than he wished things had gone different.

Me too.

So tired – need to get some sleep.

- *Jed*

August 28th   *Integrity will not feed you.....*

I have been thinking a lot about what happened out on Hwy 72. I feel I screwed up. No matter how I look at how wrong those peoples views are – I may have single handily cost lives in the neighborhood. I could have agreed to work with them – for a time period. During that time we could have exchanged services for goods. Maybe that is precisely how they were viewing it as they knew our neighborhood was not all white and they were willing to sacrifice their own beliefs.

<u>Crap</u>. Not sure if there is anything I can do about this.

I set up several "traps" out back behind my fence to see if I could catch some rabbits like Eric did. With some of the spare wood we have some pens could be built. If I can get a couple of females and males in a month or so we could have more – and when they get old enough, even more. This could be a great way to get us through the winter as far as meat goes. We have some small chickens that we hatched from the chickens Ben gave us. Will keep trying to increase their population as well.

Should have thought about the whole rabbit thing BEFORE we shot so many of them and lowered their population down.

Kenny and I are going hunting tomorrow. I have not been able to figure anything out as far as preserving the meat. I don't have the expertise to smoke it, dry it, and not so sure about canning it – though that may be a possibility I could try. I don't have a pressure canner.

While sitting outside in the dark tonight I asked M if she was happy. She looked at me and said that she thought that was a strange question to ask. I told her I wanted an answer- an honest one. She told me that she is very glad we are together. She is glad that it is me she is with as the world is crumbling around us. She also said she wished The Event had never happened – but that did not mean that she wished us not together. Bottom line is The Event did happen and we are together and she is glad to be where she is.

I didn't hear a "yes" in her answer but I think I understand what she is saying.

We cuddled in the dark as the temperature started to drop. With the intense heat we have been having – the chill in the air was very welcome. It did remind me that winter is coming and we needed to prepare for that.....sooner than later.

- Jed

August 29th   Joel is a good man.....

I walked over to Joel's house this morning. This thing with Hwy 72 has been eating me up. I have always hated the feeling of regret and I very much regret reacting the way I did. Joel and I made some small talk about planned Sunday services – and the conversation made its way to what happened. I told Joel that I needed to "lay the cards on the table".

I told Joel about my feelings that I made a mistake with Hwy 72. I told him that I did not want him to think I condone racism at all – but I am thinking about what is best for the neighborhood. Joel sat silent for a minute like he was really searching for the words to convey what he was thinking. He looked at me and uttered the words......"Jed, you did make a mistake."

I was shocked. He went on to say that he has dealt with racism many times in his life. Sometimes he put up with it because it was in his best interest to just be quiet. Sometimes he did not stay quiet. He said that I overreacted and failed to look at the big picture. He appreciated the gesture – but the entire neighborhood needs to come first. Somehow I wasn't feeling any better.

We talked for awhile longer and I headed back home. I talked to M about the situation and told her I want to try to make it right. I am going back to Hwy 72 and see if I can get things right. She is supportive and said she wants to go with me.

We'll see what tomorrow brings. Hopefully it will benefit the rest of the neighborhood.

- Jed

August 30th   Hwy 72 visited.....

I woke up this morning, watered several of the plants out back from the
rain barrels, and checked the rabbit traps. Awesome!!! I caught one – a
male (or more accurately I guess they are called a Buck). I placed it in one
of the pens I built out of some deck wood. It is basically a large box using
the ground as the bottom and bird netting over the top for protection
from predators. The fence around the back yard will keep some critters
out – we'll see how well it works. I need to build something to raise the
rabbits off the ground like Eric did which will make capturing the rabbit
pellets easier. The garden could use them.

Around 10:30am M and I headed over to see the folks over on Hwy 72. I
pulled up to the front entrance and it was guarded now. I pulled up and
the man walked over carrying on old pump action shotgun that likely has
taken many birds over its lifetime. I told him I was wanting to speak with
Phil and Lisa. The guy yelled up to one of homes and Phil and came
walking down over the hill. Once he saw M and I – he motioned to let us
through.

Phil walked over to us in the Jeep and said he was surprised to see us. I
shook his hand as I stepped out of the vehicle and told him that I wanted
to apologize. I explained that even with the world ending around us -I am
still human and can make mistakes. I told him that I was hoping we
could still talk about our neighborhoods working together for the benefit
of both. He said that he would like that.

I felt relieved as M squeezed my arm knowing how this had been
weighing on my mind.

We walked over to a small overhanging carport-type shelter where two
men stood. These were older men in their late 50's or early 60's. Farmer
looking types to be honest. Their names were Jack and Mitch. They
talked to me about their farm – cows, chickens, goats – even two small
catfish ponds. They said they have had very few problems
with trespassers but felt that it was just a matter of time. They have

weapons – but not much for firepower. They have heard of the violence going on across the country – especially in cities. With the limited travel that a few of the farm hands have done they saw evidence of the violence and desperation out there. Bodies lying in the street, houses burned down, rapes, and kidnappings – Jack, Mitch and Phil continued that they have many resources but are in need of help with security.

I told all of them that I appreciated their time and I apologized for my previous departure. I told them that we needed to work out some details but felt that we could provide the help they needed.

Over the next hour we hashed out the details of our agreement. I told them that upon approval from the neighborhood I would return the next day to begin fulfilling our end of the deal.

M said she was very thankful and said that the people seemed awfully nice. I told her that looks can be deceiving but they did seem OK. Phil and I had a private conversation when he led me to an outhouse. He said some of the residents certainly had some seriously negative opinions on anyone that wasn't white. He said a few others were not as bad and were changing and more accepted. Phil told me that he did not share their opinions – but he married into the family. Regardless – he said they were good people.

My hand is getting tired of writing.

- Jed

August 31st   Neighborhood meeting.....

I asked M and Aaron if they could walk the neighborhood and inform everyone of an important meeting today at 2:00pm at the model home. I was surprised to see M, Aaron AND Jessie – with her little girl Addie about 1 hour later walking together. M and Aaron came back home and I asked how everything was. She said just fine. I inquired how Jessie was doing. M said she seemed fine and mentioned that she needed to stop feeling sorry for herself and mingle with the neighbors again. I thought of Mark and my anger toward the Blue Bandanna Gang started growing. I still want revenge.

Regardless – I was happy to see Jessie out and about. I went and charged up my portable DVD player using the battery bank attached to my solar system. I asked M to take it over to Jessie for Addie so she could watch a movie. In today's world – that 2 hour kid's movie is such a huge treat for a little girl. It was the least I could do.

2:00pm came and many showed at the model home. As everyone gathered around I spoke of my trip to Hwy 72 and the opportunity and conditions that were in front of us. I admitted my mistake and explained my efforts to rectify the situation.

I described the agreement that was hashed out and needed their approval to move forward:

- We would provide <u>6 people</u> to live 1 week at a time to assist in patrolling and security.
- These patrols would be fed and provided shelter.
- The patrols would have to be armed for defense and security.
- In return for our assistance -
  - Each week we will receive 4 chickens, every other week a rooster for a total of 8 weeks.
  - At the end of each week the returning group to the neighborhood will bring back two dozen eggs, a block of cheese and up to 12 catfish.

- o   After 2 months we would receive 2 pigs,
- o   After 4 months we would receive 2 cows
- o   After 6 months we would receive 2 more pigs and another cow.

At 6 months everything would be reevaluated. To sum it up- if we help for 6 months we would have 32 more chickens with 4 roosters, 600 eggs, 192 catfish, 16 blocks of cheese, 4 pigs, and 3 cows.

This would be a lot more than we have now and would be a big step in a direction of self reliance.

When I finished many were chatting. I asked if there were any questions and several asked at once who would go. I answered that I felt that volunteers should work. If we failed to get the volunteers – the deal would be off. At that point I asked for a show of hands of those in favor of the deal. Most everyone raised their hand.

I thanked everyone and then said that the hard part was next. I needed 6 volunteers. Silence engulfed the crowd. I told them that I need 6 people to travel just a few miles away, live on the farm, assist in providing security and defend their land if need be.

One hand went up – it was Mike from the other side of the neighborhood. He has 6 kids along with his wife. I asked for another and there were no hands. Mike stood up and told the crowd that we needed to do this. He said that people are hungry with limited supplies – this was a way to improve our situation. Neil raised his hand, stood up and declared – "I'll go!" Then Tommy from around the corner. Brian as well who lives near Mike. Kenny then stood up and volunteered. Silence once again fell over the crowd. An awkward moment was interrupted when Joel stood up and raised his hand. "Yes" – Joel volunteered. I asked him if he was sure and he said confidently – "Yes."

I thanked them then Ryan and I met with the group of six shortly thereafter. We decided that tomorrow morning they would be taken for their 1st week on the farm.

I am so hopeful that this works out.

- Jed

September 1st *Six of our own head out.....*

This morning Mike, Neil, Tommy, Brian, Kenny, and Joel headed out to Hwy 72. Prior to leaving Ryan and I went over what everyone was bringing with them - especially firearms.

Mike had no weapons of any kind.

Neil had an old Winchester 1300 Defender 12 gauge shotgun with a Sidesaddle shell holder.

Tommy had a Mini-30 semi-auto rifle along with a Ruger GP100 .357 Magnum revolver.

Brian stood there holding a nice Ruger 10/22 with a Hogue stock, bull barrel, and some brand of scope sitting on top.

Kenny carried an AR-15 – a full size A2 model.

Joel – like Mike – had no weapons.

Joel and Mike needed something to defend themselves and Hwy 72. I handed Joel my Remington 870 shotgun along with a bag containing extra shells and a cleaning kit. I asked Joel if he had ever shot and he said he had experience with shotguns – but it had been awhile. Mostly sporting clays. Bill arrived and handed Mike a lever action Marlin in .357 Magnum and a couple boxes of shells. Both Joel and Mike were thankful.

Before we departed Joel led us in a prayer. Afterwards families said their good-bye's and in two vehicles we headed out.

Within 15 minutes we arrived and were greeted by the folks at the Hwy 72 Farm. Phil, Jack and Mitch came out to greet everyone. Ryan had wrote up a suggested plan using our six men along with six from Hwy 72. Jack said he would take everyone to their living quarters, provide a tour of the property, and get the patrols started.

Phil walked Ryan and I to the Jeep. Just as I was about to get in – I turned to Phil and told him that I am holding him personally responsible for these six men. If anything happens to them in any way beyond the agreed responsibilities - he would be the one to answer for it. He knew I meant every word. Phil held out his hand, I met it with mine and we shook hands. Phil told me they would be fine and well cared for.

On the trip back I told Ryan I would be very interested to hear from the guys next Sunday when they come home. Now we need to see about finding six more volunteers.

- Jed

September 2nd   The trouble never ends.....

This morning a small boy on the other side of the neighborhood near the service road was attacked by a coyote. Very rare that coyotes attack humans. Maybe it was the animal was extremely hungry due to the rabbit population decreasing over the last weeks. Maybe it was that the boy was playing with his cat in the backyard. Maybe the coyote was sick or injured. Maybe a combination of all of hose.

The boys mother ran out of the house hitting the coyote with a garden hoe laying nearby. The coyote started running off before one of the patrols in a tower shot it dead. The boy will be OK – several bites. Rose – the neighbor who is in charge of the Medical Team – had to clean up his wounds and give him 24 stitches.

Another danger in a dangerous world. Glad I have a fence in the back yard so I don't have to worry about this when M, Aaron, or Caleb are out back.

Karl drove over from Walnut Street. I miss male companionship. Alright – no funny thoughts. Mark was my best friend around here. My best friend from High School has long since moved away and lost contact. I love having M here, and Aaron and I are getting along great, but I miss having a "buddy". Bill and I get along – but he listens to the radios all night and sleeps during the day. We just don't see each other that often. Anyways, Karl and I sat in the garage for a couple hours talking. I ran an extension cord from my battery bank to power a couple fans – it's HOT. Karl said that things are going OK on Walnut Street. Food is extremely rationed. A book I gave him on finding edible plants has helped a bit. He said he makes a pine needle tea every couple days – good vitamin C. He said one couple this past Wednesday overdosed on painkillers. They couldn't take living in the world that exists today. The couple used to have the latest gadgets, big screen TV's, brand new cars every couple years – and now.... all that was important to them is useless. They just couldn't take it.

Choices. You have to live with them or.....you don't.

- Jed

September 3rd   Labor Day.....

In the past, today would have been a day that many would be off from work and neighbors, friends, and relatives would get together, cook out, have a few drinks, and just enjoy life.

Not today.

Phil from Hwy 72 came to the neighborhood. There was a problem. To sum it up the Blue Bandanna Gang hit the farm. What awful luck that this happens just two days after our six arrive there. Best account looks like 12 gang members that attacked just before lunch. Six of them escaped with their life – six did not. They killed 8 people – including Mike and Neil.

Oh my god – what have I done? If I had just let everything be Mike and Neil wouldn't have been on the farm. They would still be here in the neighborhood. Mike would still be with his wife Jennifer, and their 6 children. After Phil left I sat out back behind the shed crying. All I could think about was those poor kids. Now Jennifer is alone. Now those kids have no father.

What have I done?

M came out and tried to make me feel better. It helped – a little. After she walked away and I saw Caleb and Aaron talking to M – I made a decision. A decision that I swear on my parents graves I will fulfill even if it kills me. Those evil, pathetic low-life's will pay. The blue bandanna gang will pay for the pain they have caused. They have killed Mark. They have killed Neil and Mike. They have killed countless others including those over on Walnut Street.

I am not exactly how it will be done but it WILL be done.

- Jed

September 4th   It's going to get dangerous.....

Today the Mike and Neil were buried. I told Phil they would not be replaced this week. We agreed most likely the gang that hit Hwy 72 would stay away – for now. Jennifer, Mike's wife – was absolutely a wreck. Who could blame her. Several women in the neighborhood agreed to take shifts to watch her and help with the kids. The kids. My god those poor kids.

I talked to Ryan about Hwy 72, and the Blue Bandanna Gang. What a corny name for a gang but I don't know what else to call them. As far as Hwy 72 it will be difficult to find volunteers to fulfill our agreement I suspect after what happened. We decided that Thursday we would start campaigning with everyone in the neighborhood to find 6 more to go for another week.

Now – I brought up the gang and the need to do something about them. Ryan agreed. While we were talking Bill came over and got in on the conversation. I told them that the gang was a threat to all of us and they will continue to wreak havoc in the area and will no doubt hit us again. Any success they have will lead to their numbers growing. We need to hit them and hit them hard. I then told them a quote that I had memorized years ago:

> *"Injustice anywhere is a threat to justice everywhere."*
> - Martin Luther King, Jr.

Both Bill and Ryan agreed it was time.

We need a plan. The decision was for the three of us to regroup tomorrow and bring ideas on how to do it.

I suspect M will not be happy.

- *Jed*

September 5th   Finding their headquarters.....

Bill, Ryan and I decided to see if we could find where the gang had their headquarters. We took the Jeep out and headed to what was generally considered the "bad" part of town. We were all nervous, and we were heavily armed. I wore an inexpensive tactical vest I had bought a couple years ago. With it I had my S&W M&P9 9mm pistol, four extra magazines plus one in the pistol, six 30-rd Magpul PMAG magazines for my Stag AR which road beside me along with a couple more in a pouch on my belt. Ryan had his Mini-14 and extra magazines. Bill had his Mossberg 500 along with a pouch full of extra shells. We all hoped no shots would be fired today.

We headed down Saluda Street. Many houses were burned down, and lots of graffiti on buildings that were still standing. We saw an older man riding a bicycle going down a side street so we turned down to talk to him. We pulled up and scared him half to death. He turned and we recognized each other. It was Guy! Guy was one of the first people we ran into after venturing out of the neighborhood after The Event. He asked right away -"Any more peanut butter?" Bill told him no but we had a couple cans of soup and some hard candy – but we needed some information. We asked about the Blue Bandanna Gang and where they hold up. Guy smiled and I wish he hadn't. I haven't seen that many craters since I looked at the moon as a kid through a telescope. Guy went on to say that he knew of two places – an old recreation center out at Boyd Hill and an empty warehouse that used to be a Carter's Lumber. He said they stay at Carter's but spend time during the day over at the rec center. I asked how many members – he said he guessed around 30 but really wasn't sure.

We gave Guy his treats and moved on.

We drove over to the old Carter's Lumber and from a safe distance checked the area out with binoculars. We understood why they choose this location. It was surrounded with a fence with bob-wire running along the top. We could see a couple of pit bulls running around inside the fence. No one else was seen for over 30 minutes. I sketched a general map of the property and we headed home.

The three of us talked. This is where we would strike. We needed to figure out when and how – and who would be involved.

I am going to need to tell M.

- Jed

September 6th *We get some help.....*

Karl Faile from Walnut street delivered several barrels of water, heard of the problems – and offered to help. He said he also wanted to participate in the strike against he gang. I reminded him of his family and asked if he was sure. He said yes – that as long as that gang roamed unchecked his family would be in danger. I told him that I would radio him and let him know more in a day or two.

Ryan, Bill and I planned another scouting trip. This one would be at night to see the activities at the lumbar yard. We decided to go there tomorrow just as the sun went down and camp all night.

I need to tell M tomorrow what we are doing – and planning. I have been putting it off but can't anymore.

Ryan and I discussed how this was going to go down – brainstorming ideas. I said the goal has to be to reduce their numbers....drastically. We need to get information during our scouting trip and then determine positions to deploy neighborhood members. We needed to set up fields of fire to cover all exits....except one. There a sniper would wait and those trying to retreat would be taken out.

Another concern is they could wait it out inside the building. We don't have the resources to wait them out nor do we want them to radio for back up – if that is possible. The building has got to burn.

Tomorrow night we will scout the property and then a plan will be made.

Tomorrow I have to tell M.

 - Jed

September 7th   Scouting trip.....

I am writing this while Bill is glassing the lumber yard. Needed to take a break – didn't think I would have time to make this entry. Ryan is back behind a tree about 125 yards away watching the area around us. We each have a Midland radio so we can talk.

So far these idiots have no patrols walking the yard. They do have two dogs – looks like pit bulls but difficult to tell – roaming the yard. I guess they are counting on the dogs barking as an alarm.

I drew a map of the building and grounds – with entrance ways, obstacles, methods for cover, and of course windows. It is 3:00am as I write this and we have not seen any activity since about 12:30am. Between 8:00pm and 9:30pm approx 25 gang members entered the yard through the fence. A few were in vehicles, some riding motorcycles, and a couple on mountain bikes. At 10:00pm they let the dogs out to roam free.

I am not real comfortable basing our plans on one evening of surveillance. Will see what happens the rest of the night and suggest we come back in a day or two.

I told M that we were planning an offensive strike against the gang. She started crying and said she doesn't want to end up like Jennifer or Jessie – alone. I told her I had no plan on dying and was looking forward to many years of looking into her beautiful blue eyes. I told her we would plan this thing out the best we could – and hit them hard. I explained – and surprisingly she agreed – that gangs like this must be dealt with or we remain all at risk. I went on to asked her how would she feel knowing that we could have taken action against them but didn't, only to have them enter the neighborhood and something happen to Caleb or Aaron? That pretty much convinced her.

She asked when it was going to happen. Told her nothing was written in stone but Monday was looking good.

————————————————————-

It's now 4:00am – still no signs of people at the yard.

- Jed

September 8th   It's almost time.....

Ryan, Bill and I discussed going on another scouting trip tomorrow night. We have some good information on the gang at the lumber yard but a second scouting trip needs to be done.

These guys are slack and over confident. No patrols at all during the night – just their two dogs roaming the yard. We have a map of the yard, building and immediate area. They have limited exits once inside. I doubt they have HAM radio – no external antenna's so calling for back up is unlikely unless they are close by.

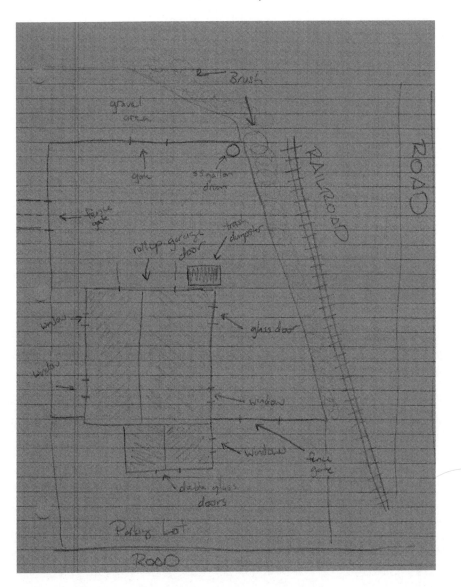

The three of us brainstormed how this would all go down based on what we know now. We figured our group would consist of 5-6 people who would approach from the southern direction.

Here are a few thoughts:

If no one is visible – two would make their way up in the brush next to the railroad tracks until they reached the northern corner of the fence. This would be **Group #1**. They would split and separate out so one person covers the rear while the other covers the western side of the building.

Group #2 would make their way to the southern corner of the fence near the railroad tracks. They will cover the entire east side and take out anyone exiting.

Group #3 will watch the entire front entrance from the east near the railroad tracks. Forgot to draw it on the map but I remember there was a broken down car just off the road near the tracks. It and its engine block could provide cover.

Everyone will have to know their fields of fire to prevent a friendly fire situation.

As gang members exit the building they will be taken out. Semi-automatic rifle fire is needed. Range is too far for shotguns or pistols.

The thing is – we need to get them out of the building. No tear gas and no smoke grenades. It has to be fire. The old Molotov Cocktail should do the trick. Thinking we will need one group just to do that – from the West-side of the building through the two windows. Multiple Molotov's through the windows and a couple on the roof as well. That should push them in Group #1, #2, and #3's direction.

Still thinking about what to do about the dogs. If they start freaking out the gang could start coming outside before we are fully ready.

The time is drawing near.

- *Jed*

I just thought of something. Something I didn't think about until now. What if there are innocent women and children in the building?

September 9th Trip to the lumber yard and folks return.....

Writing this while watching the lumber yard.

Tommy, Brian, Kenny, and Joel came back home today (feels like yesterday as I am writing this at 3:00am). It was a somber occasion as six had left but only four came back with the death of Mike and Neal and all. Another reminder that this attack on the Bandanna Gang must be done.

As promised – they came back fed and brought with them 18 eggs along with 4 chickens. Many in the neighborhood are looking forward to being able to eat more fresh eggs, meat from chickens eventually, catfish, etc.

Carrie and Jessie walked the neighborhood Friday and Saturday looking for volunteers to go back to Hwy 72 for another week. It was difficult but they managed to find six more to go. M and I drove them over this afternoon. A few guns needed to be borrowed. From what Joel said – the folks at the Hwy 72 Farm were fine. They had no issues with them. They said they ate great – especially the catfish from the pond.

At the lumber yard nothing is different. About 9:30pm the last of the gang members entered the building and no one has been seen since. It appeared that the final group of 4 men to come in had a girl with them. She had her hands tied behind her back and was being forced to walk. When they got to the door of the main building she screamed as they pushed her in. I could hear the men laughing as she screamed. My blood has been boiling ever since.

Bill, Ryan and I will be heading back home in a few minutes. Will get some sleep and then start making final preparations.

The time is drawing near.

- Jed

September 10th   Planning is over – now its time.....

The group has been formed that will hit the gang at the lumber yard.

Bill

Ryan

Kenny

Phil (from Hwy 72)

Karl (from Walnut Street)

Sam (from Walnut Street)

and myself.

I had talked to Phil about the plan when the last group was dropped off for the week. He said he wanted to be included – especially after their group had been hit. He said he felt guilty about Mike and Neil – that if it wasn't for him contacting us they would still be alive. I told him that it was not his fault and we all are responsible for our own decisions.

Karl had already volunteered and I radioed him earlier and told him that tomorrow night was it. I will pick him up around 10:00am. He said he was bringing someone as well.

Bill, Ryan, Kenny and myself got together and discussed the plans for tomorrow night. We went over the plans repeatedly and tried to consider potential problems. Dogs barking, someone coming outside before we were ready, or possible late arrivals to the lumber yard. We said that none of it really mattered as long as the Molotov Cocktails were able to be thrown as planned.

We need 3 Molotov Cocktails thrown through each of the west-side windows, along with 3-4 on the roof. We have the bottles, the fuel, as well as some Styrofoam that will be dissolved in the gas to thicken it and make it stick.

Tomorrow everyone will get together by 2:00pm to go over the plan. Everyone will have a job and everyone will know everyone else's job in case someone goes down. I spent a decent amount of time tonight cleaning and lubricating my guns. I need to be able to depend on them.

This might be my last journal entry. Tomorrow night is it and if I don't make it back, well, that's REALLY it. I talked to Eric today about what might happen and made him promise me that he would take care of M, Aaron and Caleb for me. I radioed Ben and told him that "something" might happen – and if it did would M and the kids be able to stay with him. He said yes. I told Eric I needed him to get them there. Eric promised he would – and tried to laugh it off saying nothing would happen to me.

A lot has happened in the last couple months. This neighborhood has really come together and is *surviving*. We have teams working on water, food, scouting, educating our youth, caring for the sick. Everyone looks to me as a leader – but they can move forward without me.

To think I waited all those years to be with M and tonight might be the last I will ever have with her – better make it count.

Well – hope to be writing again Wednesday. If not.........

- Jed

PS – M told me she had something important to tell me. What a tease. She said I will have to wait until after I get back to find out what it is. I wonder.....

September 11th – no entry

September 12th   I'm alive and M has big news.....

I'm alive.

What a long night last night was. We arrived near the lumber yard about 8:00pm and stayed well away. Once darkness fell we made our way across the road from the yard behind some bushes and watched.......and waited.

We went over the plan one last time. At 1:00am Karl and Sam took the box of Molotov Cocktails far to the west, crossed the road, and approached the yard. It was agreed that at 2:00am they would act.

At 1:30am Bill and Ryan (**Group #1**) headed to the brush beside the railroad tracks on the east side. They had to take out the dogs. I had worked since last night on a special surprise for the
them. Rummaging through one of the homes that was in process of being built when The Event happened I found several sizes of PVC pipe.
I constructed a suppressor that works amazingly well for one of my Ruger 10/22's. Loaded with CCI Mini-Mag standard velocity ammo the loudest part of the shot is hearing the bolt slap back and forth. Any way's - Ryan was able to eliminate the dogs at approx 25-30 yards with no problem. Left my 10/22 laying in the brush and Bill and Ryan moved on to the northern ends of the fence.

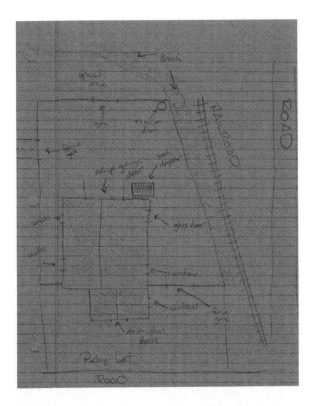

Phil and I (**Group #2**) made our way to the southern corner of the fence near the railroad tracks. We waited covering the entire east side of the yard.

Kenny (**Group #3**) watched the entire front entrance from the east near the railroad tracks. Kenny sat behind the broken down car and waited.

At 1:55am Karl radioed that they were almost in position and would light and toss the Molotov Cocktails in 5 minutes. Those 5 minutes seemed like they lasted an hour. Right at 2:00am Karl pressed the call-button on his walkie-talkie to signal their start. A few moments later I could see the flicker of light from the fire. With the power out any light could be seen easily. Next I saw the fire on top of the building where Karl and Sam threw the last of the Molotov Cocktails. They knew the plan and ran to our meeting location safe from the lanes of fire. Within moments the gang members started exiting the building. Most were all holding weapons of some kind. When they opened the door light from the fire blasted into the night. Shadows could be seen in through the windows and glass doors.

Everyone was ready. Kenny has his .270 Winchester hunting rifle behind the car at close to 85 yards. As gang members exited out the front he started shooting – causing the first to fold like a cafeteria chair. I had a bead on those exiting the east side and began engaging targets at close to 50 yards. The red dot from my Vortex Strikefire rested on moving target after moving target. Return fire from the gang started after several members went down. They just shot randomly into the dark toward the railroad tracks. Out the front and the east-side a few hoodlums exited on fire. This really helped light up the area for continued shooting.

I heard the booms coming from Kenny as he worked the bolt on his rifle. Bill and Ryan could be heard periodically shooting as gang members exited on the northern side. The vast majority exited the building on the east side in mine and Phil's direction. Phil shot his borrowed Mini-30 and I my Stag M4.

The whole event seemed to last a long time but in reality when I quickly looked at my watch it was only 2:12am. There was a large explosion inside the building followed by several smaller explosions. A large section of the southeast corner of the building was blown out and the roof collapsed. I am guessing propane tanks might have been the cause. The building really started burning at this point. I estimated that I shot 12 gang members. From the look of the building and the lack of anyone exiting – I radioed everyone "BLUEBERRY!!!.....BLUEBERRY!!!" which was code to pull back to our meet up location.

By the way – one of M's favorite fruits are blueberries. That's where I came up with the code.

Everyone made it fine. Everyone did what they were supposed to do. Going over the plan time and time again paid off. We retreated back approx 400 yards to where we parked the Jeep and headed home. We estimated 28 killed by each persons account. We don't know exactly how many were in the building but no doubt the Blue Bandanna Gang received a devastating blow tonight. The glow of the fire burning could be seen miles away.

I was not sure how I would feel after. I feel...... relieved. I am relieved it is over. I know there is more evil out there and no doubt that evil will visit the neighborhood at some point again. We have more work to do. We will be ready.

Everyone was very happy to see us return safe. M squeezed me harder than she ever had. I reminded her that she had something to tell me. She whispered in my ear "a little later". Eric was there and mentioned that he told me so that I would be fine. I just laughed. Jessie walked up to me and gave me a hug and said *"Thank you Jed. Thank you for getting justice for Mark."* Tears came to my eyes as I nodded.

M and I drove the Jeep from the model house to our home. OUR home. I like that. Aaron and Caleb were there and ran over and hugged me. It was great.

We ate breakfast as the sun started to come up. We had pancakes and powdered milk....again. Glad I stocked up on A LOT of syrup. After breakfast M and I walked out back in the backyard and sat in some chairs under some trees. We commented you could feel Fall coming as we noted the lower temperature of the morning. We talked about everything that has happened since the night of The Event. So much has changed.

I told M that I have had enough change to last a lifetime and needed "No more!" M tugged on my arm and looked at me and said that she hated to burst my bubble but there was more change coming. I asked her what it could possibly be?

M said...... *"I'm pregnant."*

- Jed

ABOUT THE AUTHOR

John Rourke is the owner of several websites including
1776PatriotUSA.com, AmericanExitStrategy.com,
FreePrepperEbooks.com, SeasonedCitizenPrepper.com, and
PrepperSeedBanks.com.

Rourke is married and has two wonderful boys – and two awesome
husky's(Jake and Bella). Living in the Southeastern United States he enjoys
gardening, shooting, mountain biking, and spending time outdoors.

Printed in Great Britain
by Amazon

34990760R00073